THE BOOK OF BARCELONA

The Book of Barcelona

EDITED BY
MANEL OLLÉ & ZOË TURNER

Part of Comma's 'Reading the City' series

First published in Great Britain by Comma Press, 2021.

www.commapress.co.uk

'An Exemplary Life' was first published in *Plantes d'interior* by Empúries (2011). 'The
Santa Anna Hotel' was first published in *Barcelona Suites* by Univers (2019). 'Flags' was
first published in *La força de la gravetat* by Quaderns Crema (2006). 'Ester (without an
aitch)' was first published in *És que abans no érem així* by Columna (2020). 'Atoms Like
Snowflakes' was first published in *Cavalcarem tota la nit* by Proa (2019). 'Guardians of
Contemporary Art' was first published in *Barcelona Suites* by Univers (2019). 'Speed
Queen' was first published in *Puja a casa* by L'altra Editorial (2014). 'Every Colour' was
first published in *Anatomia de les distàncies curtes* by Periscopi (2016). 'Other People's
Partners' was first published in *Las parejas de los demás* by Mondadori (2012).

A CIP catalogue record of this book is available from the British Library.

ISBN: 1910974056
ISBN-13: 978-1-91097-405-6

This work was translated with the help of a grant from the Institut Ramon Llull.

The publisher gratefully acknowledges the support of Arts Council England.

Contents

CONTENTS

Introduction

WITHOUT STORIES, BARCELONA wouldn't exist as we know it. In fact, it wouldn't exist at all. That may seem like an unwarranted exaggeration, but it isn't. No city would ever quite be a city if it was unable to imagine itself: if it didn't accept and project a long flow of ever-changing fictions. At most, we'd have a shapeless – albeit relatively orderly and inhabitable – mass of houses, people, vehicles, parks, and monuments. Barcelona, like every urban conglomeration, only begins to deserve the moniker 'city' when stories circulate through its streets and its keyholes, stories capable of enumerating all sorts of versions of its history, predilections, and moral texture.

Not every story in this flow of fictions carries the same weight, not every one will stand the test of time, not every one ranks as literature. There are persistent infiltrators found in every city: mercenary accounts, manoeuvres of distraction, and concealed advertising campaigns. Swirling amidst the various constellations of discourse each offering their version of the city, there are always a few that strive, in vain, to define the city, instead of telling one of its stories. And there are always some that challenge these authoritarian attempts to exclusively control the city's 'image'.

Luckily, in this battle between local visions, we also have true literature, always swooping in to complicate things, to contradict and deprogram – wholesale or piecemeal – the one-note slogans and portraits that those in positions – real or aspirational – of power (political, academic, media, economic) brandish in an attempt to appropriate the city's symbolic capital. Literature worth reading and rereading has always been a strange, anti-authoritarian beast that finds a way to elude the determinism of *diktats* and department heads. But, as we all know, even the finest literature can become domesticated, forced in varying degrees to become a tool in service to the city's conversion into political and/or commercial merchandise that's perfectly wrapped, denaturalised, odourless and, with all its conflicts and sharp edges smoothed, suitable for consumption by audiences in local and even global literary superstores.

Trapped within the plains between the Besós and Llobregat rivers, between the Mediterranean coast and the mountains of Montjuïc and Tibidabo, the city of Barcelona expanded in the early decades of the twentieth century and absorbed smaller cities that are now neighbourhoods (Gràcia, Sant Andreu, Sants, Sarrià…). This geography imposes limited dimensions on Barcelona, making it very densely populated but, at the same time, keeping it at a relatively reasonable size of some one and a half million inhabitants, far from the monstrous proportions of other world capitals. However, this is somewhat of a mirage: Barcelona has expanded during the last 60 years so that its edges are butted right up against other large cities: Badalona, L'Hospitalet, El Prat, Santa Coloma. Each has their own municipal administration and their own personality, but still share the same metropolitan area.

The city's urbanistic expansion, from the initial seed of the Roman city, reveals, layer by layer, two millennia of history. The nineteenth-century geometry of the Eixample, a neighbourhood of artisans and the middle class, connects Barcelona's diverse and colourful old city with the surrounding former towns and the new bedroom communities that came up haphazardly during Francoism (1939-1975) to accommodate the massive waves of immigration, first from other regions of Spain — particularly Valencia, Murcia, Andalusia, and Galicia — and later from other parts of the world, particularly Latin America, Asia, and Northwest Africa. The city has a great capacity for incorporating foreigners.

Barcelona is the capital of a stateless nation (Catalonia), and is the second-largest city of a state (Spain) that has always regarded it with distrust, as a component that has never been entirely tamed and assimilated. General Espartero, Spanish regent and head statesman from 1840-1843, famously said that Spain had to bomb Barcelona every forty years. And indeed, for the last three centuries, this city's military barracks have been aimed not at repelling foreign invasions but at defending the city from itself: to repress uprisings and riots. Periodically they have emerged, especially in the nineteenth century and in recent times: social and national protests, anti-government strikes and reactive protests, sudden outbursts that have failed to articulate lasting alternatives. Barcelona earned its nickname as the 'Rose of Fire'; the city's resistance to sending young men to the colonial army to fight in Morocco led to a widespread protest that culminated in the rebellion known as the Tragic Week, in 1909, where anti-clerical sentiment provoked the burning of churches and convents. The consolidation of the anarchist worker's movement in Barcelona culminated in a long general strike in 1919 that led to the recognition of a 40-hour work week in Spain. In parallel, the Republican and Catalanist movements were gaining strength. The proclamation of the Second Spanish Republic (1931-1939) was preceded by the fleeting Catalan Republic, which spread to the rest of Spain and agreed to join a Spanish Republic that would guarantee its autonomy.

After the Civil War, Barcelona became a shadow of its former self, as Franco's fascist regime eliminated any traces of Catalan culture, including the Catalan language's public presence. During the final decades of Franco's dictatorship, the city became one of the primary centres of opposition to his rule, of connection with Europe, and of Catalan cultural renewal after the trauma and repression of the post-war period. During the late seventies, following Franco's death, much of the city's efforts were devoted to improving conditions in the neighbourhoods on the outskirts. However, the deficit of municipal infrastructure has never been resolved. With the hosting of the 1992 Olympic Games, the 'Barcelona model' was forged, combining a desire to attract international business and tourism. As far as tourism goes, the model has been too successful for its own good, with mass low-cost online tourism leading to the gentrification of neighbourhoods and real estate speculation that has displaced locals. Meanwhile, Barcelona struggles under the contradictions and limitations of its castrating, ambiguous condition as a cultural and economic capital that cannot entirely govern itself nor make its own decisions. The city partially adapts, partially tries to change things, and partially tries to escape along a tangent, imagining itself beyond its limits. Here we return to the importance of fiction. Barcelona does this with methodical devotion to either introspection or to posturing and rushing headlong into the future, and especially by projecting itself culturally, socially and economically out beyond the state's borders, to broader horizons. For centuries, Barcelona has had its sights set on the Mediterranean, Europe, and the globe.

Barcelona has been a literary city since the Middle Ages. Not only as a setting for fiction, but also as the birthplace and chosen residence of many great writers. Since the late nineteenth century, the literary use of the Catalan language was the driving force behind a cultural movement – both cosmopolitan and with deep local roots – that connected with the most au courant European trends of the fin de siècle. Catalan modernists and *noucentistes* attentively watched for innovations arriving from Paris, London, and Berlin. The avant-garde in Barcelona produced their own take on them.

The translation into Catalan of classic and modern books, which has continued to grow since then, is also an example of that ambition to have relevance beyond the local. The great Catalan modern authors have had less international significance than their quality would suggest, because they are written in a language with only a few million speakers and without a supportive nation-state. Meanwhile, their artist counterparts are celebrated internationally, such as the architect Antoni Gaudí, and the painters Joan Miró, Salvador Dalí and Antoni Tàpies.

The Spanish Civil War ended in 1939 with Republican defeat and fascist victory, leading to a fragmentation of the Catalan literary panorama into territorial exile and inner exile. Some of the great writers fled to Latin America, while others continued to write and create in situ despite the hostile dictatorship. It wasn't until the 1960s that Franco relaxed the restrictions on publishing in Catalan. From then on, Catalan literature, and culture in general, was able to reconnect with its audience, and make a strong and varied resurgence as one of the spearheads of the anti-Francoist movement, alongside the social and political organisations. The Nova Cançó political folksong movement had important popular repercussions within the context of new forms of mass cultural expression.

Alongside the new generations of Catalan writers, the late Francoist period also saw – for the first time in Catalonia – groups of contemporary authors writing in Spanish, a literary language that had been used before in Barcelona, but in a much rarer and more marginalised way. The new political and sociolinguistic contexts favoured this development. Those writers are now considered part of Catalan culture, while also belonging to Spanish-language literature, as do the great Latin American writers who have lived for long periods in Barcelona, such as Gabriel García Márquez and Roberto Bolaño, just as the francophone writers based in Barcelona (for example, Mathias Énard) are considered French writers.

After Franco's death in 1975, a new world of possibilities opened up for Catalan letters. New publishing houses and media outlets in the Catalan language appeared. Catalan, as the bridge language of education, allowed for new generations of readers, while consolidating the university departments devoted to Catalan literary studies, along with new institutions and platforms for international dissemination, such as the Institut Ramon Llull. Notwithstanding, its small-scale demographics and having to compete with Barcelona's reality as a powerful Spanish-language publishing and media centre, along with Spanish nationalist resistance to fully accept the pluricultural and plurinational character of the Kingdom of Spain, keep Catalan literature's visibility and projection in a state of some precariousness.

However, throughout the twentieth century, it has had a very strong short story tradition, with authors such as Joaquim Ruyra, Salvador Espriu, Pere Calders, Carles Soldevila, Mercè Rodoreda, Víctor Català, Jordi Sarsanedas, Montserrat Roig and Baltasar Porcel, leading up to the revival of recent decades when writers such as Quim Monzó and Sergi Pàmies, beginning in the eighties, ensured that short fiction is one of the most appreciated and cultivated genres in Catalan literature. The stories gathered in *The Book of Barcelona* offer a small glimpse of this burgeoning literary scene.

In 'Speed Queen', amid a story of love and betrayal, Jordi Nopca gives readers a glimpse of the social consequences of unemployment in the outer districts of the city, gender issues, and the presence of a humanised, overqualified, and nuanced immigration, in contrast with the typical negative perceptions. Carlota Gurt, in 'Atoms Like Snowflakes', reflects on the invisibility, loneliness, and neglect some elderly people face in the bustling city. Borja Bagunyà creates an over-the-top fable in 'An Exemplary Life', contrasting the size of someone's body with the cramped flats on the city outskirts, while also reflecting on the sensationalism of the media and the creation of modern myths and urban legends. In 'The Santa Anna Hotel' Llucia Ramis looks at an incomer's love/hate relationship with the city itself, that contradictory sensation of provisional belonging and partial rejection of someone born and raised elsewhere – in her case, Majorca – who has settled here; we also get a glancing look at Barcelona's safety concerns, with the thieves who often target tourists. In 'Flags', Francesc Serés uses the shipping port as the setting for a recreation of the minotaur and labyrinth myth, on the edge of the city, with its industrial life and the Roma communities depicted in a refreshingly un-stereotypical way. In 'Ester (without an aitch)', Empar Moliner leads us down into the city's grimy underbelly, in a story that literally descends from the wealthy upper neighbourhoods to the red-light districts, while also touching on questions of gender and womanhood in the context of a middle-class family in contemporary society. In 'Or the worst, but only just', Carlos Zanón deals with the delusional aspects of the city's watered-down rebelliousness. In 'Other People's Partners', Gonzalo Torné reflects on the city's international interconnectedness, with a protagonist trying to readapt to Barcelona after a long stretch living in London, while reflecting on various romantic relationships whose moral positions reflect sociologically significant traits of Barcelona's young, up-and-coming professionals. In 'Every Colour', Marta Orriols depicts a sensual discovery through an encounter between established Barcelonians and temporary expats. Jordi Puntí's story, 'Guardians of Contemporary Art', begins in a downtown museum to set up a tale of obsessive neighbours in a district on the outskirts, the location of a conceptual art action.

The stories that comprise this anthology were written in the last two decades by authors who are mostly of a younger generation. Although these stories cannot possibly claim to be a complete portrait of Barcelona, they certainly reflect many of its essential traits. As a whole, the book demonstrates precisely that resistance to pigeonholing: the resistance to offer a single narrative. These tales tend to reflect intranarratives, shunning the collective epic still present in society and in the social and national mobilisations that have rattled Catalan and Barcelonian society since the 2008 recession and the beginning of the most recent independence movement in 2012. In some of the stories we find a reflection of Barcelona's limits, as well as its projected image of an open, permeable, cosmopolitan, and touristic city: we come into contact with the poor outskirts, with the expatriates, with immigrants, tourists and natives returning to the city after living elsewhere. In other stories, we see the tensions of social stratification, reflected in the comparison between the centre and the periphery, or the uptown versus the downtown. Above all, we find the city's apparent ability to transform itself into a tailor-made, mythic, media-propelled image challenged by fiction.

Manel Ollé
Barcelona, September 2021

Translated from the Catalan by Mara Faye Lethem

Ester (without an aitch)

Empar Moliner

Translated from the Catalan by Peter Bush

SENYORA ESTER — ESTER WITHOUT an aitch, she always emphasised — Batet Alomar, one of the members of the team that had isolated and cultivated mother cells of the colon, emerged on the porch of their detached house (on the ground floor). She'd just arrived from work, and before heading to the swimming pool to say hello to her family, she went up to the dressing-room (on the middle floor) and put on a bikini.

'Hi!' she shouted. 'It's so hot!'

She said that so very cheerfully. Her husband and daughters were clinging to their coloured noodles in the swimming pool.

'You've knocked off really early today!' muttered her husband, from the water.

'Yes, even bacteria and microbes need a holiday!'

She always cracked that kind of joke. A pleasant, yet self-effacing joke about her own work. A joke that made it seem natural for her to be a scientist, a woman among men, and all that. Her daughters didn't twitch a single facial muscle. Her husband smiled dutifully (he too was a scientist, but was now a team-manager).

When they first met, they both cracked that kind of joke. They'd ring each other and ask after the inhabitants of their test tubes. But that was a long time ago.

'Hey, girls, don't I get a "hello"?' she complained.

1

'Hello,' said the younger fourteen-year-old. The older sixteen-year-old said nothing.

'Have you been quarrelling?' she asked.

'No, why?' responded her husband, over-egging his shocked tone.

'Well… As Emma can't even manage a "hello",' she moaned.

'Emma…' her father prompted.

'Hel-lo!' grunted her big girl.

'And aren't you going to ask me how my day went?'

Hubby and the girls were already on holiday. When she finished, in the last week of July, they'd go to Thailand. She'd organised the trip. Her husband and girls didn't even know the name of the nature park where they'd sleep and rent bikes.

'How did your day go?' asked her little one, adopting the blank tone of a robot carrying out orders.

'It was great! What do you want for supper? Are you hungry?'

'Fuck, you stress me out…' snapped her big girl. And she stuck her head underwater, and zigzagged, like a fish suddenly dodging a reef.

'I'm not,' said her husband. 'Are you?'

She'd taken a helping of quinoa to work. She was starving.

'You bet, I've eaten next-to-nothing. What about you?'

'We went to McDonald's,' said hubby.

'There were greens and fish at home,' she griped. 'Yesterday we agreed…'

Going to McDonald's was akin to being unfaithful.

'Well, you know, we didn't feel like cooking. You can if you want…'

'I'm going to get a glass of white wine,' she retorted, upset.

Why did she say 'white' when they all knew that was her favourite tipple? Why did she announce what she was going to do, if it would be obvious to the three of them? She was annoyed her husband never cooked what was in the fridge, unless *he* had bought it. If she bought fish, it would end up going off. If, on the other hand, he bought it, he'd cook it straight away. She sometimes bought haricots and, the day after, he'd buy chard and cook it. She wanted to cry.

She went up to the kitchen, on the top floor (the house was on three floors, though it was narrow, because the architect – as she put it – made the most of the mountain) and extracted an opened bottle of white wine from the fridge. Her hubby didn't drink, and she begrudged him that. If they went to a restaurant, he'd order Coca-Cola or, at most, a beer. He showed no interest in wine. She'd have liked them both to sign up for a wine-tasting course.

'It's so hot,' she repeated as she returned with her glass of wine. She'd spent the whole time driving along the motorway thinking about that moment: arriving home, the automatic entry, the swimming pool (that cost them 50 euros maintenance in the winter months and 100 in the summer), the anti-mosquito candles; their standard of living.

As she walked back, she noticed footprints on the living-room floor that led – through the French windows – to outside. She was irritated they'd left them there, because it was the day Florencia cleaned and one should respect her hard work, but decided against making another scene over the wet patches. She put her glass of wine on the teak table (to match the floor around the swimming pool that was also teak). She still didn't feel hot enough for a dip, so she decided to water the pot plants. She switched on the hose and carefully slithered it between the loungers (also made of teak). She stopped by the Swedish ivy that always thrived, then by the little cumquat tree.

Then she saw they were holding back their laughter. She turned around.

'What's wrong?' she asked, grimacing painfully, wanting to find out but also afraid of the reasoning behind their spiteful laughs. She remembered school: 'What are you laughing at?

Out with it, so we can all have a laugh.' What teacher hadn't said that?

'Nothing!' replied her big girl, as if it was an insulting question.

Her hubby plunged his face into the water.

'Come on, what's so funny?' she asked, laughing as well.

'Nothing at all, Mummy!' shouted her little girl tetchily.

'All right! All right! So nothing's wrong!' she replied, looking more than incredulous. 'You're not laughing at anything. A joke, a… Nothing at all.'

Silence descended.

'Would you like me to leave?' she asked.

'Ay…!' wailed her husband.

'Well, maybe, you know, Mummy, if you have to be so touchy?' countered her little girl.

'Touchy? But I asked you why you were laughing and you refused to say. That makes me think you were laughing at me.'

She said that, so they'd say, *no, no way,* but their expressions gave them away.

'*Were* you?'

'No,' protested her husband.

'Daddy, we were…' confessed her little girl, with a laugh.

'No!' said her big girl. 'We weren't laughing at you, we were simply commenting on your appearance.'

She emphasised 'appearance' like an actor in an American soap, and, because she exaggerated, the word sounded like a wilfully posh euphemism that was quite out of place.

Ester – without the aitch – Batet Alomar, suddenly felt very naked in her bikini. True enough, it was loose on her, because it had given after being washed so much, and, true enough, pubic hair was visible, because she'd not depilated properly.

'And what were you saying, if you don't mind?' she asked, now feeling quite limp.

4

'We can't say,' interjected her husband.

'Why?'

'No reason.'

'But what were you saying?'

'Mummy, you'll get angry,' said her big girl, as if scolding her.

'I'm angry anyway. So you might as well...'

'It was nothing, it was only a joke,' repeated her husband. 'Why don't we forget it? Jump in and have a swim, please?'

The girls laughed when they heard him.

'Why were you laughing' she asked, as if it wasn't a question. As if she'd said: 'I'm not hungry today.'

'Mummy, you're not of an age to wear that bikini. Your bum's got a lot of cellulite,' her young girl chided. 'That amount of cellulite isn't normal.'

Ester – without an aitch – Batet Alomat wore leather blousons and designer jeans (that she bought in a cheap outlet which sold soiled clothes from shop-window dummies) and shoes with studs. She liked to dance to disco music, and all the mothers at the girls' religious school (not because they were believers, they always emphasised, but because of its educational standards) said she was like a girl, just another girl, and so amusing and up for anything. Clothed, she was attractive. Naked, far from it.

'And who said that? Was it you?' she asked her husband.

She looked at him. He was gently swishing his hands this way and that in the water, like a windscreen wiper. He was sulking, like a kid caught in the act. He was a very thin man, and sunburnt as a hiker.

'Did you say that about me, Marc?'

'I didn't say "you weren't of an age", because, of course, everyone is of an age to do whatever they want in life, that goes without saying.'

Of course, *that goes without saying.* Words fit for a manager.

'But you did say I have cellulite?'

She was also expecting a *no*.

'Well, do you see, it's only natural for all mature women to get cellulite.'

It's only natural, mature women. She suddenly understood the idea behind nature. Nature ensured men could reproduce till the end. But not women. Women had to be replaced. And if necessary, they could be replaced by their daughters. That was what cats, dogs, rabbits and deer did. At some point, in a nature without conventions, that had happened with humans too. A father admired his daughters, he had to protect them against other predators, as he had protected her, at the start. But that was unnecessary: she had cellulite. As a scientist, she could understand the most instinctive habits of the species, while practising the most civilised ones. At some point in human evolution, males possessed roughly, and at another, stuck it in even more roughly. She had enjoyed being possessed, being drilled. For someone so intelligent it was a pleasure to be an object and not a subject. She'd looked down from on high, like an omniscient narrator, like the consumable, desirable object she had been. And now she was that no longer, being abandoned was much more violent than being possessed. That woman was still her, but she no longer had the packaging. Her hubby couldn't be incestuous with their daughters. Her daughters couldn't be incestuous with their father. But one way to replace that instinct was to annihilate her, to isolate her like the mother cells of the colon. Oh, her two daughters were so pretty! Much more than pretty, they were firm! What she saw in them, from the cellulite of her bum, was something fresh. The idea of a freshly picked apricot next to wrinkled, sun-dried fruit, the scent of freshness beside dank stench. The father had to laugh with his daughters, because he no longer had feelings for her, not even pity. To laugh with his daughters was to pay homage to himself; his daughters were his work. Yes, hers as well, but he could ignore that. Not even divorced fathers noticed their daughters resembled their exes, whom they hated so much. Dressed, she could still be a thing. Stripped naked, she was nothing. She spent money on shoes, handbags, lipsticks, and depilated increasingly strange places. But stripped naked it was like she wore a baggy skin she could pull over her head, right on top, and knot there. She had to get away from that swimming pool. But to do so, perforce, she'd have to display her bum's cellulite.

'Come on, jump in,' said her husband.

'No, she won't now, she's angry,' lamented her big daughter.

It was as if a dense, pink cloak of rather shameful grief had fallen from the sky and covered her. A heavy cloak of sticky, tacky candy floss mired her skin and hair and took pity on her, because none of the three aquatic beings in her household showed any. Her eyes filled with tears, not prompted by cellulite, but by her daughters' soft toys, the big one's Marie Curie and the little one's Pierre Curie who'd played leading roles in the lives of all four of them for ten years. 'Mummy, I can't find Marie', 'Mummy, Pierre Curie is hungry.' She went into the kitchen (white with warm touches, like the blackboard and the second-hand glass cabinet), opened the fridge (two doors) and gulped down the wine. She thought that drinking straight from the bottle, and not from a Riedel glass from the set in the cabinet, lent an epic and equally trite tone to that moment. She thought about their drive to the Basque Country when the kids were five and three, in two little seats, about that field of sunflowers where they stopped so Clàudia could puke, and the songs she invented (that they all remembered perfectly) so they learned the planets. She relished her tears:

'Mercury and Venus, Mars and Earth,
First, second, third and fourth.'

What a pleasure it was to sing as you sobbed!

She downed another long swig of wine and, suddenly, felt drunk. Since the menopause, she got drunk much more quickly, no longer gradually, as she did once, now it happened immediately. That layer of triteness moulded her cellulitic body. Pompeii suddenly came to mind. All four of them had gone, and she'd been moved to tears, but her hubby and kids hadn't. Those negatives of the dead, those moulds, showed no trace of cellulite. What would hers be like? A mass of wrinkles?

She recalled the now distant time when she still saw her hubby as someone sexual, the time when he didn't sleep on the sofa, because he wanted to hug and protect her all night long. Another swig. 'Down the hatch, down it goes,' she told herself. And that phrase, which was so right for a shallot feast and so wrong for a scene like the one she was now performing so sincerely, made her laugh and choke. The bottle would soon be empty. Besides, she was hungry and didn't want the greens and the fish they hadn't eaten; boiling greens and grilling fish didn't go with wine and tears. She wanted a hamburger, too. She knocked back the dregs from the bottle and tottered towards the upstairs lobby to look for the car keys (the stairs had no bannister, the architect's bright idea for women who own restrained houses).

She didn't need to dress up to go to McDrive to buy a take-away, she didn't even need to look for shoes, she'd got Crocs in the car. She'd go and buy a hamburger from McDrive, without leaving her car, and would drive straight back.

She opened the garden sliding door with the remote and thought it took too long. The car was under a wood and bracken shelter. She put on her Crocs, started the car (they wouldn't hear her from the swimming pool), switched on the left sidelight, swung right and out onto the road. It was a straight drive to San Cugat. She'd been to McDrive thousands of times, except now she was drunk, and finding it hard to think straight. She wanted a hamburger and chips she would eat at home with more wine. She looked around at the backseat, just for a second, to check the two little seats weren't there or the two little kids sitting in them, each with her own doll, Pierre or Marie. Two or three seconds, just enough to hit a streetlight. The airbag shot out and something fell on the windscreen that shattered like a mandala. When she saw what it was that had fallen down, Senyora Ester − without an aitch − Batet Alomar burst out laughing like a witch. It was a political propaganda banner. The political party leader's face − she couldn't remember his name − in that solemn, eternal stance, looked like Dracula.

'Let's beat it!' she shouted. And she touched her head.

She didn't want the police to come and test her alcohol levels, and, above all, didn't want her husband and two girls to be forced to fetch her from the police station or hospital. From hospital? Had she hurt herself? She thought not. She wasn't losing any blood, the airbag had worked perfectly. Where was she going? She couldn't remember.

She put her Crocs back on, grabbed her handbag, alighted through the rear door (the front one wouldn't open) and walked down the road away from the car.

'I can't ring home,' she shouted now.

If she rang, she'd have to say she was in her bikini, exposing all her cellulite. Neither her hubby nor her kids would want to come and get that mass of cellulite; they'd ask her to call a taxi, as they found her embarrassing. And how would they react when they discovered the car had been abandoned by a streetlight draped in a political banner? They'd have a go at her. They'd say she should go to a shrink or that they should get her put away. And once they'd said that, perhaps all three would kiss, back in the swimming pool, and gently grope each other. No. In fact, they soon rang to ask her where she'd got to. She rummaged in her bag for her mobile (luckily, she'd not left it behind), switched it off and threw it on the mountainside.

She heard the wail of a siren. The police come quickly when you don't need them! She must hide or they wouldn't let her go and get her hamburger. That was when she remembered! The hamburger! That was what she was going to do. Buy a hamburger, but where? She ran. The road was deserted, it was getting dark. She walked towards the mountain and went very quiet.

'The woods are so well kept,' she said. 'Evidently, they have a budget for that.'

She stretched out on the dry grass and closed her eyes. The two baby seats, it suddenly came to her, were in the junk-room. One was green, the other was red. She'd refused to give them away. Perhaps she'd sleep for a while. Then she'd go to McDrive, which fortunately wouldn't close till the early hours. A tear rolled from her right eye. An intrepid tear, she thought, that jumped from the bridge of her nose and segued onto her lip.

She was woken up by a mosquito bite and struggled to think where she was. Had she been there long or a little? She crouched down and perched her bum on her ankles, that – she was amused to recall – some people called 'rabbit's bellies'. At least it was still night-time. She brushed off the blades of grass and pebbles that had stuck to her body and saw how her left leg and arm were covered in marks from the bracken. She started walking down the road. Although she was still wearing a bikini, she could maybe call a taxi once she reached a village. Or maybe she'd find a bar that would make her a pork and cheese sandwich (that she also liked a lot). With bread smeared with tomato. Pork and cheese, warmed up, with bread and tomato. She gripped her handbag.

A van honked.

'Hey!' she cried, in shock. 'Watch out, you idiot!'

But then she understood that she was the one who should

be watching out, because she was walking down the middle of the road. The few cars that drove by hooted or said things. Naturally, she thought, she was wearing a bikini and Crocs.

'And it's dark, so they can't see the cellulite,' she muttered. And she wiped her eyes, which kept watering. She couldn't tell whether the excess of emotion she always showed had nurtured that flood of tears or whether she showed an excess of emotion because her tears came in floods.

'Maybe I'd better walk along the verge,' she shouted. And she started singing.

She came to the look-out point. Full of lads and lasses, holding bottles or cans of beer, sitting on the stone bench and watching the city lights.

'Now I know where I am!' she said. And nodded, because she realised that she'd gone downhill, towards Barcelona, the opposite direction to where she wanted to go.

'How small the Sagrada Família is,' she remarked.

'Fucking hell!' shouted a young lad when he saw her. It sounded like 'Forkin' 'ell!'

'Can you give me a drop of beer?' she asked. She avoided the word 'mouthful', which seemed too twee for that situation, but 'drop' also seemed too lady-like.

A lad gave her a can from his little ice-box. She opened it and gulped it down.

'What? On the job?' he asked.

'Yes,' she replied. 'No.'

'What do you charge?' he asked.

'Wait a mo',' said Ester – without an aitch – Batet Alomar. And she finished off the beer.

'You were thirsty, right?' the lad shouted. The others gathered around them.

'Where's she come from?' asked a lass. 'Are you all right?'

'She's on the game,' he replied. 'I expect she usually works here.

'On the game,' she thought. So she was on the game now.

'What do you charge?' asked another lad.

'Leave her alone, you idiots,' the lass lambasted them.

That made her laugh. That girl could be her elder daughter. Indeed, her elder daughter would have reacted sympathetically like that (towards a stranger). She sometimes went there, to the Tibidabo look-out point, with her friends.

'I'm very hungry,' she said.

'Do you want something to eat?'

'Have you got a McDonald's?'

They all laughed. The lad grabbed her shoulder gently, as if he wanted to take her somewhere.

'For fuck's sake, Toni!' the lass protested.

'She's working. It's a job like any other!' he defended himself.

'That's exploitation, exploitation of women!' she bawled. 'You're filthy!'

'It's a job like any other,' said another of the lads, all spotty-faced. 'She's working.'

Senyora Ester – without an aitch – Batet Alomar thought they were about to launch into a debate about whether prostitution should be legalised or not.

'I won't charge much, because I've got cellulite,' she said.

'Don't be silly, you're lovely,' responded Spotty-Face. 'What's your name?'

'Ester, without an aitch.'

'Come on then, Esther without an aitch,' said the lad Toni.

All three walked towards one of the parked cars.

'Toni, Pau! For fuck's sake!' shouted their friends.

'Do you want to work?' asked Spotty-Face.

'Yes!' she cheerfully replied.

All three got into the backseat of the car. They sat down. Their friends protested.

'Don't video this, right?' said the lad by the name of Pau.

And he addressed her: 'It's your call.'

She laughed. It had never been her call when it came to sex. What should she do? Go down on them in turn? Maybe.

'Unzip,' she told them cheerfully.

She got on with it, with one, then with the other, thinking her own thoughts, with no feeling, wondering at herself, and finding relief in nature's predictable mutations. Now the penis of the lad on her left swelled, now the lad on her right shut his eyes, now both were moaning. Once she'd finished off both of them, Spotty-Face took out his wallet.

'I've got 20 euros. Will that do?'

'I'd like to go to McDonald's,' she replied. 'Yes, 20 will do.'

'Do you want us to drive you there now? Can you wait?'

'No.'

'But which McDonald's do you want? The one in Plaça Catalunya?'

'Yes.'

She didn't remember there was a McDonald's in Plaça Catalunya. Maybe because of the accident or because she was drunk.

The lad Toni got out of the car and told his friends he was accompanying the woman to Barcelona. The others shouted to him. He came back with two beers.

'Hey, do you want one?'

She grabbed the beer and opened it. She sat in the backseat and let them drive. Spotty-Face was driving.

'I've never done anything like that before,' said the lad Toni.

'Me neither, guy, me neither,' the other lad replied.

'Me neither!' she chirped.

She put the 20 euros in her purse, and leaned her head on the window. 'What would her family be doing now? Had they called the police or were they still in the swimming pool?'

She got out of the car and thanked them. There was a Burger King and a McDonald's on Carrer Pelai, near La Rambla. Maybe she'd go to Burger King?

'Are you all right? Have you got a place to go?' asked Spotty-Face.

'I'm good.'

She went into Burger King, queued (there were two people) and asked for the set deal and a beer. The server, a girl her older daughter's age, didn't seem at all fazed to see her in a bikini. She paid with the 20-euro note and waited in a corner until they called her. She walked into the street with her sandwich wrapped up (she'd asked for a take-away) and sat down on the Zara stone doorstep. She took a bite. She was so hungry. Then they snatched her handbag.

'I can't catch the train now,' she reacted.

She carried on eating, quite blank-faced, and the second she finished she walked down La Rambla.

'It's great not worrying you might be robbed,' she exclaimed.

The promenade was full of tourists, some on the tipsy side. A man touched her bum.

'Hey! Pay up!' she shouted.

The man rushed off.

She turned down a side street leading into a Plaça Reial packed with tourists. She thought how the square's closed-in space made voices echo a lot. She leant against a wall for a moment. A man wearing tergal trousers immediately accosted her.

'How much?' he asked in English.

'You're Catalan!' she screamed. 'I can tell from your accent.'

'Quan cobres?' he then asked, as if he'd not heard her. He didn't want any chit-chat.

'20 euros,' she replied. 'No, if it's only you, that'll be ten.'

She thought everything she was saying was witty, but nobody laughed.

The man took a ten-euro note from his wallet.

'No condom,' he stipulated.

'No way. I've got the menopause and can't fuck without lubrication. I'm totally dry. If you want, I'll give you a blow-job.'

'Where?'

'I don't know,' she answered. 'Where does one go? What do the city statutes say?'

The man shook his head and went as if to move on.

'No, wait!' she shouted. 'I was joking. What about an entranceway? If you want to go to a pension, you'll have to pay.'

They went down Carrer de la Lleona, which was completely dark. He gave her the ten euros and unzipped. She kneeled down. Where could she put her money now?

'I see I need to invest in a handbag,' she said. But the guy didn't even laugh. Such a poor sense of humour.

The man's penis reminded her of a mushroom, and that made her think how few adult penises she'd seen in her lifetime. Four, all told. Her husband's and three others. No, there were the two lads from just now!

She got on with it and, finally, spat it out, on the sly, so he wasn't offended.

'What's the time?' she asked, once she was back on her feet.

He took his mobile from his pocket.

'Nine minutes past three,' he said.

'It's late! Long past my bedtime!'

But the man had gone.

'A whore that says "long past". I'm pissing myself.'

And she burst out laughing.

'I *am* literally pissing myself!'

She crouched down and pulled down her bikini bottom, as if she were in the mountains, which was the only place she'd ever peed without a toilet bowl underneath. She didn't have time to finish. Someone poured liquid from a plastic bottle of water on her from a window. She immediately registered that it was piss.

'Filthy cow!' they shouted down.

'That's absurd!' she exclaimed, looking up. 'You're pouring pee on me because I'm having a pee.'

She walked slowly off, dripping.

'I bet I stink.'

And then, while wondering whether to go back to the square to a wash in the fountain in the centre, she ruminated over the fact that the Catalan language had a word for a good smell, *olor*, and another for a bad smell, *pudor*. It smells, it stinks. It was a good idea to go to the fountain. She only had to make sure she didn't lose the ten-euro note while she splashed herself. But she couldn't find the square, or ask anyone if they knew where it was, because the moment anyone saw her and caught a whiff, they ran in the opposite direction.

'A poor man!' she shouted.

A man was sleeping on a mattress in a porch.

'This guy won't be offended by the stink,' she muttered.

She lay down next to him. The man didn't stir. There was a box of wine by his bedhead.

'He did without the Riedel glasses,' she said. And laughed and laughed.

The man opened his eyes.

'Eh? Quién eres?' he asked in an accent she couldn't place.

'Ester,' she replied. But it wasn't worth telling him it was Ester without an aitch; that absent letter aitch now belonged to a life that was no longer hers. The man gently took the ten-euro note in a way she thought quite magical, and tucked it inside his trousers. He immediately curled his hand around her shoulder and made space for her on the mattress. She stretched out and shut her eyes. If she wanted to eat tomorrow, she'd have to work. She'd better rest now. She hugged the man who didn't complain. She smiled before going to sleep, exhausted, thinking how they were united by their stink.

An Exemplary Life

Borja Bagunyà

Translated from the Catalan by Jennifer Arnold

HE WAS BORN WEIGHING ten pounds three ounces and was, by turns, the cutest little thing, Cardona's first child, Marina's nephew, the king of his house, the bravest of all, the boy who'd had a growth spurt, the tallest in his class, the biggest boy I've ever seen in my life, a suspected case of elephantiasis gigantism, the cause of some worry to his parents, a beanpole, an ostrich, a poor creature, a case of neither gigantism nor elephantiasis, the subject of an investigation, the headline on all the front pages of the city's newspapers, holder of the Guinness World Record for the tallest and heaviest human and the giant of La Guineueta, this year's sensation, Martí Cardona.

We first came across Martí in a tabloid newspaper that featured the boy-mountain in a rather unfortunate photo shoot. The boy-mountain taking up an entire two-seater sofa. The boy-mountain holding a basketball in each hand. The boy-mountain lifting a fire extinguisher with the little finger of his left hand. He wasn't even two years old and when you saw his innocent smile, you didn't know what to make of him: was he a threat, a promise of a better future, or just another in a long list of oddities? At five feet tall and weighing nine stone, during one of his many childhood checkups he had the experts divided; was it acromegalia or elephantiasis? Those in the first group told those in the second that they'd start to consider elephantiasis when they found some kind of obstruction in the lymphatic arteries, or a reason why a boy from La Guineueta would have come into contact with filariasis. Those in the second group told those in the first that they'd never seen a case of elephantiasis on record as clear as that of Martí. *Not yet*, the others thought and, wanting to be the ones to put their name to the first, would turn up at the Cardona's house and happily offer to take over the boy's case (and his mother, when she heard them use the words *case* and *situation*, would listen politely for a brief moment before escorting them to the door, thanking them for their trouble but sure they'd understand).

During that period, Martí would hardly ever leave the house. Or rather, it was easy to think he hardly ever left the house, although now I wouldn't be able to tell you why. I suppose that a five-year-old child capable of knocking over a horse with a flick of his wrist was not easy to control. Every now and then, some curious person would stop outside the building he lived in, but I don't think anyone actually went to talk to him. I mean, what would you ask a giant? And a five-year-old one at that, as there was never any sign that the extraordinary development taking place inside his body was happening in any other way. At that time, Martí was exceptional both for his size and his simpleness. It seems he did go to school, where I suppose he had to put up with things no one should have to put up with (but I'm merely supposing as I don't actually know, and I've never found a way to confirm it; I could be wrong, and maybe Martí's body protected him from anything the others could have inflicted upon him).

When he turned twelve, and it started to seem impossible that he wasn't suffering from some kind of disease associated with or as a result of his growth, Martí must have been deeply convinced, not so much of the fact he was different, but that he was so terribly strange, and he started to understand why people didn't want to get close to him (he would even make excuses for them: it was stupid to think that they might, who on earth would want to be with someone like him, and other such things). If anyone contradicted him, or accused him affectionately of exaggerating, Martí would just point to his arms that were both more than a metre long, or his thighs that didn't fit in the chair (to sit down he had to cover the dining room with a load of cushions that were a palm-width deep and measured one metre by 80 centimetres which, in relation to his body, created the effect of nothing more than a rug that, at most, softened his contact with the floor). It's easy to think that this gesture would be enough to immediately stop everyone talking, that it almost seemed as if that's the way it had to be, that it couldn't be any other way (although the problem with Martí was that he stopped being what he was too quickly and became pretty much nothing at all, forgotten by the newspapers and always remembered by halves, always with the feeling that we knew too little about him).

I met him once, before I got to speak to his parents, although I doubt he'd remember because I don't think he even realised, we didn't even speak. In fact, we didn't really meet each other. I saw him one morning from a distance, walking around one of the city's biggest parks, and I went over to see if it was really him, along with about ten other people. He must have been more than ten feet tall. His back was like a wall and his neck like a bull's. He was with his mother, who came up to his wrists, and he was being careful not to knock her with his arms which swung as he walked. I thought about running up to him and asking him for a photo, like so many others who were standing next to him, posing with the V-sign. But then I saw myself sitting in someone else's house, looking at one of these photos they'd shown me so I could see something incredible, and being incapable of saying anything else but *Jesus, he's huge! The son of bitch is enormous. The guy's a fucking wall.* That kind of thing. People still tend to cling to the anecdotal part of the boy-mountain and, to some extent, these stolen photos feed this kind of tedium and prevent you from thinking of anything else than how big the kid was. So, as I watched his vacant gaze in front of so many cameras, I decided I didn't want to be one of those people, but rather I wanted to do more, or maybe less, I don't know.

Maybe it's just as gratuitous and commonplace as wanting to go against the majority, but at that point I realised that there was something in Martí that distanced him from others, a kind of self-absorption, or his body turning in on itself, as if it were the author of a work that doesn't know when to bring it to a close, and that work was the boy himself. I later found out (or rather, when his parents appeared in the restaurant and I dared to ask them if that's who they were and, for some reason, they told me) that same feeling had ruined all his relationships (that is if you could consider a conversation with the doorman or the type of polite chit-chat he would exchange with his mother's friends when he came across them in the kitchen, relationships). He was always overcome by a kind of undefined discomfort that eventually became unbearable. It would start as an interference, an irritable note that left many of the social gestures Martí attempted – a hug, the offer of a meal, the promise of a phone call – hanging in the air, with no resolution, as if Martí was not only Martí but something else, a kind of background noise that unsettled his interlocutors and made them leave early with a quick wave and a *see you later*. His disproportion won out at the expense of social contact and imposed itself as a priority, and no one likes to feel second best, his parents told me, and I understood.

Martí wasn't news for very long, if at any moment he had been, and his story became hidden from view; a domestic matter, a kind of half-formed question that no one really answered. It wasn't until he turned nineteen and surpassed 80 stone in weight that the neighbours on the second floor began to notice that the structure of the building was starting to weaken (although according to his mother this wasn't true, a building can support that 80 stone and much more besides, the problem was that they didn't like the shape the weight came in, prejudiced sons of bitches, she said). They were alarmed by a crack that was flirting with a pillar and creeping towards the ceiling, and so decided to speak to the Cardonas and tell them that maybe they should think about doing something. That they should do something. That they should leave. The crack was the manifestation of a fear that had been bothering the neighbours since they first heard the words *giant* or *gigantism*. The logic of this fear, however, was based as much on their lack of trust in the building's structure as it was on fantasies in which giants wore tights and breeches and were defeated by valiant knights fighting for the hand of a princess. For that reason, even though the Cardonas insisted on covering the costs of any imperfections through their insurance, a meeting was soon called in which the same problems were repeated. They couldn't bear the noise. They'd found cracks everywhere. If things carried on this way, they said (and by that they meant if the monster, whatever he was called, carried on growing), who knows what would happen (and by that they meant that the building would collapse; it was the neighbours from the two apartments on the second floor, those from the first and from the mezzanine, who were most worried about the future of the stairwell and who refused point blank to refer to him as Martí but rather *their son*).

The building's administrator, who'd had time to contact the builder, decided to put his faith in the structure and said that, according to the facts, there should be no problem at all. But what if he jumps? Or slips and falls over? Said the lady from the second floor, these things happen, and the building, it's the building that can't cope. It would be a never-ending round of hammering and fucking drilling and it would mean the end of my siesta, she said, but it was inevitable, they had to extend the doors and knock down some of the walls. The best thing for everyone would be for them to move out to the country, where there would be enough space for Martí not to be as much of a bother as he seemed to be in the city. Even though size was relative, his mother said, it didn't matter if they took him to a waste ground or an industrial unit, the problem was that they didn't have enough money to leave.

As a temporary solution, they suggested moving Martí to the ground floor (that used to be a corner shop more than three metres in size and had a door that led out onto the street), and the Salinas up to the third floor. The exchange would mean a whole load of paperwork, but Senyor Salina immediately realised that if they saved themselves the bother and Martí ended up destroying the apartment while it was still in his name, nobody could guarantee that the good faith of the Cardonas would continue. If they were going to do it, they should do it properly, he had said, but everybody thought it was more a question of when rather than how and that, deep down, everyone could find enough reason to trust the Cardonas (especially because the possibility of watching the building collapse beneath them weighed heavier than the interests of Senyor Salina, and because somebody opportunely remembered the story of the brother-in-law of someone's cousin who swapped their apartment with his sister without anybody even knowing).

Martí's second appearance in the press was the result of a combination of factors, the most important of which was a journalist whose need to fill the summer news drought dragged on to the first week in September. An error of judgement led to him salvaging the story of the enormous boy from the archives and deciding that, ten years later, it would be of interest to his newspaper's readers (or rather, to the supposed reader of the paper's summer editions, stupefied or more sensitive to stupidity than the rest of the year and willing to reread something that was more or less the same but different). The fact that the interview and photoshoot Martí was subjected to was read by the September reader amidst an effervescence of news, new cultural releases, and the return to politics since the end of July, sent certain hierarchies of information into confusion, and Martí's case was no longer seen as a mere curiosity in the lifestyle pages but an example which had a certain symbolic ascendence for the coming year. What should have been read and then forgotten became unexpectedly fixed in the reader's retinas and, after a few days, as tends to happen with cases that connect the two poles of a collective anchor, a slow proliferation of articles, opinion pieces and letters to the editor began to appear and continue for a good while – perhaps too long.

I don't remember exactly what they said, but I do know that everything was said: that Martí was an example of how technological evolution hadn't eliminated biological evolution; that it should be understood as a warning against the excesses of engineering; that the only significant thing about Martí was an absence of significant traits. Martí was perfect for any kind of metaphor. The opposition read it politically and criticised the government's lack of action, their inability to find a solution to the need for social assistance for someone like Martí. Others presented him as a challenge to the current executive that would demonstrate both their capacity to react and the privileged attention they offered to citizens, although everyone spoke about Martí as *someone like Martí* and referred to his measurements as a *case* they had to *deal with*. His story was read as summary of the classic question of whether the interests of everyone should be prioritised over the interest of the individual, or if one thing didn't necessarily oppose the other. In the majority of cases, Martí was seen as a problem (the need to create infrastructure, what should be done if there were more like him, the sacrifice he represented for a society with more serious problems) and, often, turned into spirited media protests (so we have to start rethinking the measurements of everything now? Widen the roads, make doorways bigger just in case one day Senyor Martí decides to pass by? Those kind of idiocies) which only served to show that the columnist was defending, as with so many other things, the right to keep things just as they were.

But no, Martí was a son like any other and he would be a man like any other, his parents said, almost to convince themselves that the problem lay elsewhere, that it lay with the others, without elaborating any further. Faced with that cancerous spread of opinion and critical analysis, Martí's state of mind became ever darker, especially when he was asked about the future. Martí had always refused to think about himself in terms of *usefulness* or *service*. His relationship with the world had to be different, he said to himself, and he would mutter something about finding a job in which his size wasn't a defect or a virtue, without specifying what this job was or asking himself if it even existed. When he imagined his future, he did so with the modest imagination of a person who measures five foot ten, wearing the clothes of someone who's five foot ten, in tiny offices for people who are five foot ten, or better still, thinking of H. G. Wells' *The Invisible Man*, going through the long list of film adaptations or ideas of miniaturisation, extreme forms of camouflage or those tiny pieces of clothing that don't reflect the light.

Martí took advantage of the fantasy of invisibility to avoid everything and everyone, at a time in which his case had become part of the city in a way that nobody could have predicted. He had become a category through which the city thought about itself, an argument that was invoked during discussions around tables in hundreds of cafes, and that inspired graphic designers and publicists, city poets, authors and singer-songwriters, both amateur and professional. He was a human version of Snowflake the gorilla, one of the points on the imaginary skyline that is evoked when someone asks where you live. The problem was the continuous influx of calls to the house, the invites to participate in television programmes and the infinite variations of the fifteen minutes of fame that his mother saw as a crude way of ridiculing Martí and turning him into a spectacle. Just like anyone who has to face an audience for the first time, Martí had to judge his ability to put up with the hundreds of casual looks, and he discovered that this ability was incredibly limited. Occasionally, when a gang of curious people gathered beneath his window, he would slowly raise one of his enormous hands, wait long enough for them to take a photo and then retreat, but he had little more to offer than that.

If it hadn't been that Martí never ever complained about anything, they could have won themselves some time, but that night they went to bed without saying anything they wouldn't normally say on any other night. Martí didn't realise that his pain was sharper than on other nights, nor did he hear the loud crash of a wall falling to the ground. His legs had grown at such an unusual rate that they had taken over, in both length and width, the little space that was left in the room after Martí had stretched out. Without waking, he had curled up and adopted the strategy of a nine-month-old baby pressing against the wall of their mother's uterus, but the pressure had reached an unsustainable point and, at around five in the morning, the wall at his feet gave in and his legs plunged towards the kitchen. As the wall collapsed, Martí's left leg advanced towards the door that connected the kitchen with the dining room and became wedged in the door frame that led to his parents' bedroom and the bathrooms. His mother woke his father but there was nothing they could do: Martí's leg was blocking the hallway and inflating like a balloon with every beat of his pulse. They had to leave through the window that opened from their room onto the stairway's interior patio and, from there, make their way out of the building and re-enter through the door on the street. Meanwhile, Martí's right leg, which was bent and pressing against the constraints of the apartment, found a bit of respite in the living room. As for his arms, only the right one had found a way to breathe and was now hanging out of a window and onto the pavement with veins like tubes of violet rubber; Martí's left arm remained squeezed against his body.

They realised the seriousness of the situation in the precise moment their son's body stopped inflating. With the help of his parents, Martí managed to free his head from the corner it was squeezed into and push it out through the opening between the building's metal shutters. They immediately called the emergency services and anyone else they could think of who could help, and his mother quickly started to organise the few neighbours who had been woken by the collapse of the first wall (a couple of shelving units full of jugs had also fallen, as well as the cupboard where they kept all the plates, long before the first water pipe had become trapped between the brickwork and Martí's knee), who were now running around fetching drinks and thinking of a way to stop Martí's arm from hanging downwards from the window (in the end his father moved the car and parked just below, so his arm could rest on top of the vehicle and his blood could flow more easily). Neither the fire brigade nor the police could offer a useful solution. Martí couldn't move, he was entangled in the apartment like a snake in a plastic labyrinth, and the only thing they could do was knock down the walls and partitions that weren't part of the original structure and see what happened, they said, and his mother gave them permission to do whatever, as long as they got him out of there.

An hour after the first alarm, they decided to evacuate the building. Martí's thighs were trapped between a main pillar and one of the building's central walls. In theory, it shouldn't be a problem, they said, but if Martí was to expand a tiny bit on either side, the structure of the building could be compromised. They also discussed his feet, and his hand that was now bigger than the window frame. If they didn't create some space, the blood wouldn't be able to flow up past his wrist and, if it took too long to get him out, gangrene could start to set in. Only if it took a lot of time to get him out, his mother said, but it turned out that knocking a wall down wasn't that easy and they couldn't use dynamite or any other explosive as it could put Martí in danger and yes, they had requested a demolition truck, but it hadn't arrived yet and they weren't entirely sure that would work either. By the time they had convinced more than half the residents to leave the building, taking with them as little as possible, half a dozen journalists had turned up with cameras and lights, picking neighbours at random to question (a tax inspector, a writer of instruction manuals for printers, a secondary school teacher) to find out who was who, and what was actually happening. The cameramen ran up and down the street trying to capture the enormous hand resting on the Fiat, the agitated movement of Martí's chest as it rose and fell in the tiny space permitted beneath the ceiling, and his head as he stared at the sky, not knowing what to do to get himself out of the space that had become a trap (but above all the noise, the breathing of a beached whale and those groans, those timely cries, as Martí's body pressed against the building's structure without a crack). All they got of his mother was her tearful face and, of his father, a fixed stare on Martí's final scream as he twisted dangerously against the walls that, until then, had allowed him to breathe. In horror, he ran to the entrance of the building followed by Martí's mother and the only firefighter who wasn't knocking down walls.

From the building came the sound of wood creaking or an egg slowly cracking, and it seemed that it was either his legs, someone said, or his arms being crushed, and suddenly they all started doing whatever they were doing even more quickly. Martí's body started growing once again and this time the building wasn't giving an inch. His mother realised straight away: they were taking longer to create spaces than Martí was taking to fill them. The group of firefighters who were working on the mezzanine had managed to free his left foot, which was now resting on the landing, but the rest had to stop their demolition work when his immense body decided once and for all to embark on another growth spurt and his stomach, his chest, his shoulders and all his extremities that were curled or wedged into every corner of his home, were thrust further than the floor of the building would allow. There was nothing to be done. Slowly, the rafters were burying themselves into Martí's Adam's apple.

The next morning, the press coldly reported the death of the Giant of Horta, the hope of so many. Reactions to the news were varied. From regret or necrology to those who only remembered that they'd already started to forget about him. The debates around what Martí meant for the city started up again, but in whispers, as if there wasn't a lot of sense talking about something that wasn't news. However, what they all did seem to agree on, just before they decided to give the subject up, was that they should celebrate the incredible resistance of the building, a model, they said, that should be used for all future building in the city.

The Santa Anna Hotel

Llucia Ramis

Translated from the Catalan by Laura McGloughlin

THE FIRST TIME I set foot in Barcelona was in 1991. We were coming back by van from Italy, where we'd visited some relatives, and the following day we would catch a boat to Mallorca. We came in via the Meridiana and I thought that it was the ugliest avenue I'd ever seen. Along the sides of each apartment block, dirty green awnings rippled above the clothes hanging on the balconies. I imagined the sad lives passing behind those windows that were made to rattle by the motors of cars driving into the city.

'Look,' said my mother as she raised her index finger from the steering wheel, 'that must be the Hipercor where there was that terrorist attack.'

It vaguely rang a bell. I was ten when it happened. The words 'terrorist' and 'attack' were usually linked to Madrid, where we would travel twice a year to see my grandparents; car bombs were always exploding there. For that reason, I was scared of going to Madrid as a little girl. Later, I think I got used to that fear.

My brothers looked to the left for a moment, but instantly they were back to concentrating on the Game Boy. My father was trying to work out on a map how to reach Carrer Santa Anna – a cross-street between the Ramblas and Portal de l'Àngel – because that was where the hotel we

31

would spend the night was. We went around the Christopher Columbus monument a couple of times, and before taking the Via Laietana, my father warned: 'If any time you come to Barcelona, don't hang around that area alone. It's very dangerous.'

He gestured towards the sea, or towards where the sea supposedly was. The sea wasn't visible. My father was saying something about some barracks or other, a dirty port; he was babbling from memory. As a young man he'd studied mathematics in Barcelona, but he enjoyed himself too much and failed everything, so my grandfather made him come back to Palma. For that adventure in the early sixties – demonstrations, a hippie vibe, chicks and cigarettes – he retained an idealised nostalgia about which he spoke to us less than of his military service, and an image of the dark and dense city that kept its back to the sea like someone turning their back on the world. It would become modernised in record time, but in 1991 it was still only a vague outline of what it would be.

We arrived at the hotel in the early hours of the afternoon. It was grey and depressing. Despite the street being pedestrian only, they let us park in front of the entrance to unload the luggage. We were distracted for a moment. My brothers were putting the suitcases in the lift, my parents must have been talking to the receptionist, I'd stayed in the van looking for my Walkman which had rolled under the seat. No one saw anything. The sliding door of the van had stayed open. People were passing with the energy of a post-holiday working day.

Then, my mother asked: 'Have you taken my bag?'

Raising my head, still on my knees between the seats, I saw her lean inside the van and rummage through my brothers' jumpers. She turned back to the guesthouse and repeated her question: 'Which of you has taken my bag?'

'Sweetheart, don't scare me,' said my father from the lobby.

'I'm not scaring you,' she responded, ever more impatient.

'It was here a second ago, now it's not.'

'Let's see. Have you checked the front seats? Or your glove box?' insisted my father as he came over.

'I never put my bag in the glove box,' she answered. 'We've been robbed.'

My father opened the glove box.

'It's not here.'

'Of course, it's not there, I just said I never put my bag in the glove box.'

'It has to be somewhere,' said my father.

'I'm telling you it's been stolen.'

'It can't be. Are you sure you didn't leave it at the motorway rest stop?'

'Why is it so hard for you to believe that we've been robbed?' I asked with my usual insolence.

'You stay out of this,' answered my father.

My brothers also came over. And the receptionist. My father ordered my brothers to go back inside immediately and keep the luggage in sight.

The receptionist was a weedy youth with the same shabby appearance as the hotel, or so I deduced from what our mother told us later in private: 'For sure he was in cahoots with them'. She'd also tell us: 'This is the last time we're going to a two-star hotel.'

'What's going on?' asked the receptionist.

'Our bag has just been stolen,' answered my mother, adopting a local accent.

'Well, we don't know. The bag's nowhere to be found,' specified my father, always so fair.

'Shit, Papa. It's obvious we've been fucked!' I added.

'That's enough!' my mother let fly.

'But what have I done?!' I shouted.

'You've been robbed just now?' the receptionist asked stupidly.

'Right now. While we were unpacking the suitcases. I left it here, and when I came to look for it…'

'And you didn't see anything?' said my father, addressing me.

'No, as if it's my fault!'

'I'm not saying it's your fault. I'm only asking if you saw anything. You were in the car.'

'Yes, Papa, I saw a guy come, grab Mama's bag and calmly take it away, but I didn't tell you because, you know.'

My mother was muttering: 'The cash is the least of it. The problem is the credit cards, the ID card, the return tickets…'

'For the boat?' asked my father.

'No, the lottery tickets. What do you think?' I contributed.

'Enough already! Do me a favour!' concluded my mother.

I got out of the van and strode into the hotel. My brothers were guarding the luggage like two dunces, and I told them.

'We've no tickets or money to go home. We'll be staying in Barcelona forever. From now on, we live here.'

Joan had just turned eleven and he asked, very scared: 'Has all our money been robbed?'

I was nearly fourteen and moody. 'Yes, and the credit cards too. We're poor now. We'll have to beg and live on the street.'

Miquel was eight and he wanted to know what begging meant.

'Look, you'll be singing 'Twinkle, Twinkle, Little Star' so people will give you change. You have to put your hand out like this.'

He opened his eyes wide and they filled with tears.

'But I don't want to sing. I don't want to beg.'

'It's not true! All our money hasn't been robbed! You're a liar!' shouted Joan.

'Ask Mama and Papa, and you'll see,' I answered with a nasty smile.

My father's plan had been to show us the flat belonging

to that woman who used to rent rooms on Carrer Diputació, where he lived during the time he was in Barcelona. And he also wanted to take us to the University of Barcelona and for a stroll on the Ramblas. But we spent the whole afternoon in the police station on Via Laietana, waiting to be attended to file the complaint. And then we went to the Transmediterranean office, where we had to buy another five tickets for an arm and a leg.

My father said: 'I don't understand. You have the list of passengers for tomorrow, you'll see our names on it, I'm showing you a copy of the complaint we have just filed right now. Why do we have to pay again for tickets that have been stolen?'

At the ticket booth, there was an anodyne man, the typical man you would expect to attend a ticket booth. As a little girl, I used to think that you were put through the hatch of the ticket booth when you were a baby and could still fit. Then you would grow inside, unable to come back out, and you were condemned to be a ticket-man or ticket-woman forever after.

The man answered: 'Because imagine what will happen tomorrow if five people come with the tickets you say have been stolen. We'd have a problem.'

'But no one will come with our tickets tomorrow, because they're ours.' My father was taking his wallet from his pocket. 'And here you have my identity card to show that I am the person who comes up on that list.'

The ticket vendor, who no doubt didn't know a life was possible beyond the ticket booth, looked at my father's identity card suspiciously: 'And how do we know that the others are also the ones on the list? In other words, how do I know that they are them? We can't take the risk,' he said, shaking his head in refusal.

For that man, there were unquestionable laws of the universe that had to be adhered to scrupulously.

'Then what's the solution?' said my mother in a tone that sought to be conciliatory but was absolutely incredulous.

'Buying new tickets,' the ticket vendor decided, as if we hadn't understood anything.

We were exhausted by the long return journey in the van from Italy, and we were also in very bad humour; me worst of all, who in the prime of adolescence wasn't a model of patience or sympathy. So my father paid the scandalous price of those last-minute journeys and we ate dry sandwiches in some bar near the hotel for dinner.

The room, which I was sharing with my brothers, was as gloomy and sad as that infernal day. I thought I wouldn't be able to sleep but I passed out. I didn't know it then, but from that first encounter, Barcelona would always do her utmost to make me hate her. She wouldn't manage it. I'm stubborn and I like challenges.

I'm also a romantic, even though it's taken me two broken marriages to figure it out. This is a very tough city to live in without love. The whole time she's rubbing your solitude in your face. No matter whether you live in the gay left Eixample or lively Gràcia, in boring Bonanova or gentrified Horta. I have never come to feel like I am from here, despite living here more than half the time I've been alive. Twenty-three years since I arrived here at eighteen to study and then stayed on because one thing led to another, and suddenly before I knew it, I'd married and got a mortgage I would never finish paying because I wouldn't put up with the pressure of enduring until death us do part.

Afterwards, you know, we repeat the pattern. We fool ourselves into thinking the previous attempt has given us experience and we've learned to compromise, this time's for real. I want to do things right, I said to my second husband, let's not rush. It's also a fact that the economic crisis forced us to go at a different pace. Unlike my first, who belonged to the last generation that would make money from architecture, the second was of my generation and taught philosophy classes in a school. We couldn't have bought a flat even if we'd wanted to. He'd inherited one from his grandmother in the Sagrera area that I decorated with the taste permitted by a regular wage with no expenses or children. Not that we didn't try to have kids. We did, many times with different methods. But maybe it was already too late, according to a tactless gynaecologist who insisted that after a certain age everything is more complicated.

'I was in the process of a divorce and had to focus on my work to pull through,' I'd have answered back to her, were I still the adolescent I'd been. I've learned to bite my tongue, not to be so foul-mouthed nor so vehement. A question of survival, I suppose. Or I no longer see things so clearly. Perhaps it's true the city has defeated me, little by little, expelling me. True, it's never been friendly. She was never welcoming; she puts you to the test the whole time. You have to show her you deserve her. Somehow, I was expecting the same thing of my partners, like a little princess ready to marry the knight that kills not one, not two, but seven dragons. First, I demanded that they love me madly. Then I begged for it. Now, on the verge of begging for any kind of love while singing 'Twinkle, Twinkle, Little Star' with my hand out, I've realised a pause is required.

I like to go up to the Parc del Putxet and look at Barcelona. She doesn't feel mine. Yes, I can hear the murmur of cars, which make the windows of flats no longer inhabited by locals, but by passing tourists, rattle. There is a building – a whole building in the heart of the Eixample – that has been converted into a storage facility so those who have to move can leave their furniture there. People who no longer have a home rent a chunk of an uninhabitable flat to stash their belongings. It's absurd. It's savage.

But I've also become a bit like her; like Barcelona, I mean. I've evicted the men who have inhabited me, not for any concrete reason, but because I was becoming too high-maintenance. In leaving, they left me empty, with some memories gathering dust. Bah, I'm getting sentimental when the metaphor is prettier than what happened. With my second husband, we couldn't overcome the forces that arise from wanting to have children when nature is opposed to it. We'd been the ideal couple, we even subscribed to Bicing city bikes. Then the difficulties of pedalling across Plaça de les Glòries, when we took the Meridiana en route to the city centre, became directly proportional to the difficulties we were having at home. 'What is this thing?' I would yell at him when the plants grew so tall, they made the ground around us bulge, opening unfathomably deep holes beneath our feet. We will fall in and die, you'll see, buried alive.

It wasn't always like this. A long conversation in the kitchen – they were always in the kitchen – or nights pretending to sleep while we asked ourselves if this was it, if we had to give up the dream for good to the point of making us insomniacs. It was easier to imagine that we'd fix it, and in a few years we'd laugh about all of this as we travelled with our children in a van through Europe – never staying in a two-star hotel at any point – than to accept that none of that would ever happen. But reality prevailed with timetables so as to avoid meeting at breakfast-time (he would get up early on purpose, so we didn't clash when making coffee) or at dinner (I'd come home when he was already in bed). What had become of us? We were two bodies under the same roof that kept a check on themselves so as to not bother each other. In the end, our absences, so obvious, became unbearable.

He didn't dare raise it with me, and I knew there was no alternative. The flat was his and I had always been little more than a low-wage earner of few and precarious means; searching for somewhere to live – or to drop dead – was very difficult. I'd have to resign myself to a room in a shared flat at my age, when all my friends are happily settled and have families and problems enough than for mine to be added on top. I looked for options on the web and housing apps and the results were discouraging. 500 euro for an alcove that could only fit a single bed on Passeig Maragall, 600 for a windowless hole in the Raval, 700 moving towards the Born. And who were the strangers with whom I'd have to co-habit? We've gone mad, I thought, what does all this mean? And I was happy – yes, deep down, I was happy – not to have had offspring, because what do you do if you get separated in this city and there are children in your care? Where do you put them?

Which is why I say that I had to beg them to love me. To regain my man's love so he'd let me stay a little longer – desperate – or for anyone else to love me and momentarily rescue me until I could rebuild myself and gather strength – pathetic. Or because this damned city might love me for once after so many years, and not steal projects, energy, appetite, character, time, a definite future from me time and again.

What has she done if not sucked everything away from me? 'What have you given me, you evil bitch?' I asked her from the top of Putxet. A cloud of pollution was floating above the roofs and their antennae, and the skyline was a silhouette of what she pretends to be: the Sagrada Familia, which only tourists frequent, the renowned Mapfre towers, which only tourists inhabit, the Agbar tower, which should be a hotel, and the Hotel W, which is one, as its name suggests. Beyond, the sea where the sun erupts.

In 1991, only the Sagrada Familia and the Mapfre tower existed (the Hotel Art, the clone skyscraper by the coast, would open the following year for the Olympic Games). It's shocking to think that, back then, my parents were the same age that I am now, with three children and a stability I've not found. I would think I was suffering from a midlife crisis if it were life itself and not the city that has called my existence into question. That is to say, Barcelona has defined me, but I don't fit here, this isn't my place.

I fell fatally in love on arrival, and I've since struggled to capture her attention. I've written the most beautiful love songs so that she might notice me; I've wandered her streets on foot and rode them by bike until I've known them by heart, like someone going over the name of a lover; I've forgiven her for everything, I've tried to understand her, I've hated her with all my might which is a perversion of sick love; I've wanted to flee from her, I've always come back, drawn who knows why to our devoted, unconditional and toxic relationship. I've lost the anxiety to please – the more difficult the challenges, the better. That's what kept me hooked. But what authenticity is there in that? Who are you, Barcelona? So made-up and so rough, so full of yourself and so barely yourself. You read the books and the stories and the articles written about you like someone who glances at cards from their admirers before throwing them in the dustbin, along with the bouquets of flowers.

But I don't love you anymore.

That's what we said to each other in the kitchen: it doesn't matter how long we pretend, I can't do this anymore. And every day afterwards, I went up to Parc del Putxet on foot to see if I were still capable of finding something to cling to. Even if it were only memories, that Tibidabo of old attractions we recover when the present, so full of hotels, is alien to us.

Arts is a very luxurious five-star hotel. So is the W. Apparently there are a total of twelve in the city. At least, that's what I've found on the internet. I could have spent my last night in any one of them and lived Barcelona like those who don't live or live it up there, but who leave some cash behind, no more than spare change for them. For me, it would have meant an expense that, right now, when I don't know what is to become of me, is impossible to bear. Also, I've already said that I am a romantic. I believe in signs and circles closing, in the story whose ending has meaning. Very naive, I know. And very fatalistic.

'Going? Going where?' he asked. 'You're made for the city, everyone is made for the city. The city is where things happen, and you're a junkie for things happening. You would die of boredom if every time you went out into the street there wasn't the possibility that something unforeseen might make you sidestep the itinerary you had planned, and you couldn't explain it. You wouldn't even last a year away from here.'

I didn't remember in which hotel I'd spent my first night in Barcelona. I had to consult my family via WhatsApp: Was it a hotel or guesthouse? On Portaferrissa?

My mother: 'I don't remember the name, but I think it was near Porta de l'Àngel or whatever it's called.'

Joan sent a screenshot of two photos on Google Maps. One was of the street, Carrer Santa Anna. The other was the hotel entrance, flanked by two strawberry trees in tubs. What a memory, I respond.

Miquel writes: 'I remember Mama saying that it was the last time we were staying in a two-star hotel, but I don't know if it was that trip.'

My mother: 'Yessssss! I recognise the entrance and I also remember having said that (crying laughing emoji).'

My mother another time: 'I think that was the year we bought the Nissan and we were coming back from Italy, right? It was Easter week.'

The hotel had a website, of course. How did we make reservations before? I suppose you had to go to travel agents; I myself used to have to go to them the first few years in Barcelona, every time I spent the holidays at home. How long ago, all that. From the photos, I can see that the furniture hasn't changed since we were there. They're surely the same as when it opened, but there's no information anywhere, nor any reference to its history. It's a pity, I'd like to know more about it – when it was built, to whom it belonged – and to discover its ghosts.

There's a broken piano in a room stuffed with cheap landscape paintings, moulting brown sofas, those imitation medieval chairs with lion's heads at the ends of the armrests, lights like in your granny's house, porcelain ornaments with swans on top of crumbling wood and faux-marble surfaces. On the dining room benches, there are coloured cushions to conceal the decadence. For breakfast, toast, cured meats, industrial croissants, buns, apples and oranges. In reception, an oriental carpet, an old PC in the corner and a Coca-Cola machine.

I reserve a triple room, even though I'll be sleeping there all alone. I have a hope that it'll be the same one I shared with my brothers, almost thirty years ago now.

I read somewhere that the Aymara people consider that what we have before us is the past, and therefore we see it. I think that the future doesn't exist for them. I imagine that the future is behind us, it's a stranger that follows us, we feel its breath on our necks, it makes us afraid that it might chase us. We have a tendency to turn around to look at the future and see what it's like. But if we do so, we lose sight of the past and that's when we fall flat on our face. I think about this while closing the last box, the sound of packing tape – shriek, shriek – has filled the entire day. He helps me carry it to the car. Twenty-three years fit in a Seat Ibiza, that's all that I'm taking away from them. We hug each other and he says I can re-consider. For a second I think he's going to ask me to stay, but he's only referring to tonight: he doesn't understand why I have to spend it in a hotel, if the boat is leaving tomorrow anyway.

I answer that I need it. 'I need to close this properly,' I say, or something like that. I'm romantic, nostalgic, melancholy, he'll tell me. But he doesn't. I raise my fingers from the steering wheel and wave at him through the window. I start the car and spend three hours driving around Barcelona, like a taxi driver through the locations of my life; how much these laps will have cost me.

I park the car in front of the hotel. On one side they have opened a shop selling ham. I enter the reception. I've left the car door open and my bag clearly in view on the seat, so that someone might rob it and steal my identity, my tickets home.

Flags

Francesc Serés

Translated from the Catalan by Helena Buffery

'ALL CALM AT SEA?' Dexeus from time to time asks the lads at the security desk. And they always say yes, the sea is dead calm, nothing new to report. He asks the same question with a certain regularity, only broken occasionally, unexpectedly, in order to break with routine. Afterwards, he sits down and continues to watch the same screens that the two security guards are surveying in their own office.

From the windows you can see a tugboat turning the container ship to which it is attached. For 22 years he has watched the boats coming in, but every time they make a manoeuvre, he stops to watch them play: some of them lifting their prow and sinking their propellers, like beasts raising their snouts in their determination to pull harder; the others advancing slowly, carefully tied one to the other, the boy pulling the hand of the father, the father allowing himself to be pulled and leaving his little one to do all the work. The oil tankers are even slower: the tugs wait until there is no danger or obstruction and then both of them draw on the power of each other's engines, one pulling forwards and the other backwards in a ballet that ends with them facing the tubes destined to empty, fill or clean the tanks. Dexeus watches each of the manoeuvres just as he had the very first day he came to work. His boss had sent him to the second unloading wharf, and there he saw a tug making an enormous container ship turn through 180 degrees. The solemn languor of these great hulks continues to enthral him.

In the old days, he used to have to oversee all manoeuvres in his sector, but as the years have passed the sea has become ever calmer. Since they installed the internal video security system, he has spent more time watching the video screens than the wharves. And his computer... The security firm responsible for the access points and the wharves provides an incident report every hour, on the hour. Sometimes he thinks of the years he used to spend going up and down on his bicycle, crossing the unloading zones with their piles of containers, labyrinthine and unending. Kim and Pilar, who work under him, are the ones who log and archive the reports, watching out for any warning messages, while the two security guards monitor the same screens that he does... The sea is normally calm. Every so often he even goes down to do a quick walk around without any real need to do so. Ever since he managed to cover all the entrance and exit points with checkpoints and barriers, and there's been a barbed wire fence surrounding the perimeter of the port, there are no more busybodies or thieves, and all he has to do is watch over the workers. Before, hardly a day went by without something or other happening. Someone out for a walk who had fallen into the sea, someone else who had had a bump in their car, fuel spills or broken-down ships.

Normally, the port appears tranquil. Today, however, the sea is not calm, and he may be wrong, but he could swear he's seen somebody slipping in under the fence. It was only momentary, but he's almost 100 per cent certain he saw them, that he even saw their face. Suddenly, it is as if someone had thrown a stone into a pond and all order had been broken. Vessels often get into difficulty: ferries that have broken down or fuel spillages, nothing that can't be fixed if you follow the protocols. But sometimes the sea is not calm; sometimes the sea becomes so rough that the waves reach as far as his tower. Today the sea is not calm... He'd swear a girl has slipped in under one of the gaps in the fence.

'Did you see her?' he asked when they opened the door, but neither of the guards has seen a thing, not a single thing. He has, he's sure of it: a young slip of a thing coming in over towards the road to Montjuïc Lighthouse in the direction of El Morrot. They look at him in surprise. No, they haven't seen a thing, not a thing.

'But, if you like, we can go and check it out. Right away. We'll let the guards down there know, too.'

'No. Leave it, I'll go,' Dexeus picks up the master keys and a torch. It's mid-morning, but if he has to look inside a container, he'll need light.

Of course he wanted to go himself; the girl got in via one of the areas he had insisted needed to be better protected. Sometimes kiddies get in, they make holes in the fence, small enough to be hidden by the neighbouring brush. Long ago, as Dexeus remembers all too well, they used to come in search of food, towards the waste dumps where all the agricargo that has gone off in transit or during the unloading process is thrown. They came from the gypsy encampments and also from Can Tunis, but ever since a lorry hit two children, they haven't been back... That was years ago, all that. Now there are children who come from the Polvorí area, and some from Poble Sec. Dexeus knows this because he's the one who signs the complaint forms. Before, they used to come in search of fruit and food, but now it can be anything: mobile phones, tools you'd hardly imagine them being able to drag off with them, even the odd laptop the port workers have left for just a moment. Documents, briefcases which they take without the foggiest idea of what's inside... They take what they can and hide somewhere they think no one will find them. They wait until it is dark to come out and then move from one hiding place to another until they can reach the holes they've made in the fences. Once he caught one who said, quick as a wink, that they were just playing at getting in and out, that's all, and another who claimed they were looking for treasure... Who knows the tales they tell about the things inside the port?

Dexeus comes down from his tower, starts up his motorbike and sets off towards the containers. Kim and Pilar have nothing more to say, they know all too well why he wants to go down to check for himself. Everyone knows how, long ago, a boy got in, before they had erected the protective fencing. He'd hidden somewhere on the loading wharf, in one of the gaps between two containers. They didn't find him for three days. One of the forklifts moved a pile of containers and his small body fell down from between the metal, his chest crushed. The boy had been dead for more than two days, according to the forensic scientist, and anything could have killed him: the movement of one of the containers, a sudden push from one of the forklifts, even the settling of the cargo inside. It might have been the lightest, most insignificant of blows, such a fragile body amidst so much metal. Dexeus only heard of it afterwards; he was never there on the weekends. The boy got in on Thursday and they didn't find him until Saturday, by which time everyone had forgotten about it. Now, every time they catch a thief inside the port, Dexeus immediately asks how many there are with him, if he's alone, if there are children waiting for him outside. It terrifies him to think of children running around in there. Another time, they had to go out on a launch to fetch one who had hidden on a ship.

Were it not for the fact he had seen it so clearly, he would be doubting himself right now. The guards watching the security footage haven't seen anything, nor those patrolling the port, and he is unsure whether to go towards the metals zone or the silos, the container terminals or the open wharf.

Towards the silos, that'll be it. There's lots of movement there and children are drawn to movement; they know they'll find something – who knows what – but sometimes they've had to turf them out from right there, between the hoppers and the pneumatic unloaders. There were a couple he nabbed because they couldn't stop sneezing from the soya dust.

That's where the cornflour is unloaded, along with all sorts of other grains that arrive in the holds of the ships and go up to the top of the silos, clouds of dust spewing from their gaping mouths, like enormous, cylindrical chimneys placed all in a row. As if the storage tanks were reminding everyone of their centrality, the whole wharf smells of flour… The workers haven't seen anything, not even the crane operator who has to load and unload the grain. Up there, above everything, he hasn't seen a thing; he was just watching the corn and hasn't spotted anything out of the ordinary…

Dexeus always thinks the same thing. Where would I hide if I got in here? But he knows it's a useless question, he has no need to get inside in search of anything. Where would I hide if people were looking for me? Where would I hide if I wanted to steal something? Not in the metals wharf; the parts are enormous, and everyone is careful to leave lots of space between one set of cargo and another. There is too much bare concrete. It is terrifying over there; the ginormous forklifts are the biggest in the entire port. No wonder we call them bulls – toros – here. Up and down they go, sweeping the entire quay, with huge beams on their outstretched horns. Any time they have to turn it is like they are scything the whole surface of the wharf.

Dexeus moves very slowly, stopping his bike at every building to ask whether anyone has seen anything. Everything is in order, they all reply, the sea is calm.

There is a light, temperate breeze, as if sent by the sun to deny anything can be wrong, to confirm what he hears in every office, every building, that everything is fine. Pilar then informs him that the sea is not calm, that the splashback from one of the pipes on the open wharf has spattered a ship, turning it from white to black. The stevedores cut off the pressure and the spurt becomes little more than a drip of stains which the workers are trying to dissolve with yellow foam. It's all under control, Pilar tells him from the tower. When he gets there, he finds the ship is covered from top to bottom, and there is a man shouting in some form of English full of Greek words. It is the captain who's come up from one of the stairwells to curse his rotten luck. The strangest ships come to the open wharf: hulks carrying cargo from faraway refineries or platforms, sporting flags of convenience – Liberian, Panamanian – and international crews. From the cabins of this one emerges Philipinos or Malaysians with hoses and brushes to try to clean the stains dripping down the sides, on deck, all over the ship, before they dry, while the captain continues his shouting. I'll be going home filthy, he shouts over and over in English, we'll be going home filthy.

The usual hustle and bustle, as if the everyday had expanded, adapted even, in order to include everything that happens in the port. The people who come and go, the people who are always the same and go nowhere… Suddenly, in the distance, he thinks he has seen something: someone moving around in the container terminal, someone too small to be there alone; when workers bring their children they never leave them on their own. He's glimpsed them from the corner of his eye and quickly turns towards the container wharf. He thinks they've gone down the street between the second and third berth; it looked to him that they were wearing the same clothes he saw on the security screen, he couldn't see their face clearly, they were too far away. But on screen he had: it even seemed to him they were looking at him for an instant, straight at the camera. It might be a coincidence, that they were simply passing under the wire, between the fence and the ground, face up. Of course they could not help looking up at the camera, but for Dexeus it was as if they were looking at him. Not this time. Now he just glimpsed them in the distance, and perhaps it wasn't even the same one he saw slipping through the gap in the fence.

The street separating the cargo berths is empty. The containers construct a city of metal: a perfect grid, of diverse colours and provenance, that extends out beneath the radius of the cranes. The order with which they are aligned contrasts with the uneven heights of the exterior rows and interior squares, if we can call them that. A child who wanted to play hide and seek here could spend days without anyone finding them. Dexeus informs the tower that he is at the container wharf, and that he thinks he has seen her, but there is no need for anyone to come down, just to let him know if they see a little girl on her own.

In the meantime, he begins to walk around the metal and concrete grid, the streets along which the forklifts race around like bulls, quickly, quickly, much faster than is permitted, much slower than the companies would prefer. If a child passed through here, they would surely crush her without even realising it: the forklifts move so quickly, they accelerate hard, it is difficult for them to brake and they can't always see what they have in front of them, their line of sight obscured by the cargo. There are accidents here every week, crashes between forklifts carrying containers or goods; the screech of metal against metal, the scrape of metal against cement, is blood-curdling, as if two ships were colliding. When the forklifts run over or clip anyone the results are awful... He remembers the boy who was trapped between the containers, dead.

He too has driven one; he knows how to do it, to get the fork into the skids in the container in one go, without braking. He was adept at cutting across corners without losing speed, and had also had races with other drivers to see who arrived first. How he loves them, these raging bulls, with their tonnes and tonnes of metal stuck on their horns. It is as if the driver were the brain of a beast with little need for belief. That's why he is so fearful. He knows these bulls never stop, they pick up speed and move forward inexorably, with the containers skewered on their metal horns. He can't avoid noting this; he is up at the top of one of the squares, and every so often he can hear the shriek of the horns as they deposit or pick up their containers. Dexeus goes up and down, peering at the gaps between the corrugated steel of the container walls: some are doubled over, two or three men could hide there. Up and down the container streets he goes, calling up again and again to the crane operators to see if they have seen anything out of the ordinary, someone, a child, climbing on to the containers... But everyone responds that they have seen nothing.

He even gets one of the forklift drivers to lift him up on one of the forks and ferry him up and down the streets as if to survey the labyrinth from on high. If he were the girl, he'd say that was cheating, Dexeus chuckles to himself from above the landscape of containers laid out before him, of every colour and provenance, like a child's game. Here there is everything, all the goods in the world are here. And this little runt has come in to see if she can swipe jackets or bags, he thinks to himself, as the bull ferries him up and down the streets of the wharf, him above it all, surveying the strange shapes inside the blocks, a labyrinth of metal.

Dexeus calls everyone, but no one has seen anything anywhere. In every one of the departments, they take note of the fact he is looking for a girl or maybe a little boy, and to let him know if anyone sees anything unusual. That's what they do, but no one sees anything... How small a child is, in here, between the metal and the ships that dock and then leave. Dexeus continues the search, he starts his motorbike and looks around the container grid, careful to brake at the crossroads, as the bulls would run into him without even noticing. He continues the search... It would be such bad luck if after a few hours here something bad happened to them. Maybe they've gone already, maybe they got out, but he continues to look, mindful of the places he's already visited, the control towers he's asked; he even goes up in a crane to check he can't find them. No, from there, everything is perfectly in order, but at the same time unbelievably large, overwhelming and chaotic. If they don't want you to, you won't find them; from the crane cabin you can't see anything, you have to go down below.

Back to the ships again, to the open wharf, to the refrigeration wharf and the scrap metal. Here, there and everywhere. Now is when he's lost, now that he's searching for something.

Pilar calls. Someone in logistics thinks they've seen a boy, it could also be a girl: someone with a multi-coloured bag, from afar, just enough time to see them running under one of the carriages. The agent can't stop what they are doing, they were just tagging containers and pallets, but the girl was headed for the loading zone in the freight rail terminal.

The loading zone is like a bramble field: it's impossible to get out without a scratch. The noise in the terminal is tremendous: iron scraping on iron, electric and diesel engines, fans from the refrigerated chambers and alternators that make the walls of the warehouses shudder. Everything seems to have been made precisely to ensure no one would want to stay there long. Perhaps that is why he hadn't thought of going there; if they don't want to be found, they won't be. The bulls charge over the crossings that weave across the railway tracks: impossible lines and curves that cross at the signal changes, black from grease and soot... Diagonally from the rails, Dexeus enters into a chaos of silvery grids, carriages and containers; beams and bars; machines, cranes, and forklifts racing like lunatic bulls to load up a yellow or green container, it hardly matters which. And yes, he knows that all of this is ordered, that the movements are perfectly controlled, but right now it is all beyond him. There is a little girl who can be smashed to smithereens, the carriage wheels slice like knives and he can call her all he wants, all he damn wants… She must be watching him from behind some box or other, from under a carriage that could move away at any time. Yes, he can call all he wants, all he damn wants, shout even louder, if he likes, but to no avail. She won't come out. It's when a girl gets in that the bulls become dangerous.

He stops one driver after another, and another, but nobody has seen anything and everyone curses the fact she decided to hide here. The machines return to their business the minute their operators have said no, that they'd keep an eye out, and Dexeus continues to walk along the tracks, going from one side to the other, and shouting against the roar of the machines, cursing the thought that if she's watching him now from behind a crack somewhere, from behind some wall, she must be afraid of him, and afraid of the bulls and the cranes, lost amidst all of the metal. The forklifts honk their horns to tell him he's in the way, get out of it.

One of the trains going towards logistics is loaded up with refrigerated containers; Dexeus saw them loading beef carcasses. And glass, the back carriages were loaded with glass, crate after crate of it: perfect cubes of white bottles and sheets of glass that appear and disappear without cease from the platform until they are all stacked on the carriages. But in amidst all of this he can find nothing, nothing at all… Maybe she has gone already, maybe she's followed the line of the tracks out. She may even have climbed up on one of the convoys that are leaving the station ever so slowly.

The walkie-talkie is on constantly; she is nowhere, negative responses everywhere… She has to be here, one of the bull drivers saw her. Which one? Impossible to know. By this time, he's probably in another area entirely, he may even have finished his shift... Dexeus shouts again: Come out, come out, we won't hurt you, come out, don't be afraid...

One of the convoys pulls away from the station slowly, carrying copper in large reels, flanked by wooden planks and slats. Dexeus climbs up and sits at the very top, on top of the copper wire. The train moves away slowly between the rails and the warehouses, between the elevated platforms; so slowly that from above the carriage you can now see all the places he hadn't even considered, spaces between refrigerated containers, gaps and cavities that the warehouses never close, containers that are rusting from the sea salt and display cracks and holes where you could fit almost anything, but not a trace of the girl. He informs the two security guards that he is leaving the station, that in an hour or so someone should go and fetch him from the logistics zone outside the port, as he is sure the convoy will stop there. If she has left already, this is the way she must have gone.

There you go! He sees her jump from the train, seven or eight wagons in front. She is running next to the tracks, towards the place where the fence ends. There are lots of kids there waiting and as soon as they see her, they stop playing ball and run towards the fence, too. Now he thinks it could be a boy with long hair. It's kids from the caravans on the waste ground – the encampments – from where more kids are now running towards the fence to see the train go by: they have seen all sorts of trains and convoys, but they must be surprised to see someone on top, seated high above the copper thread. Dexeus sees that the girl is dragging some sort of fabric or bundle behind her, he's not sure what, but when she gets to where the fence ends, she mingles with the others. There must be more than thirty or forty of them, of all ages.

As soon as she crosses the fence, the kids crowd around her until she is completely surrounded. It looks like they are changing clothes and passing around multi-coloured pieces of fabric. Yes, they are the same pieces he saw the girl dragging behind her: flags that the kids are passing one to the other, and which they throw up into the air, bundled up into balls, so that they unfurl as they fall. A couple of them are showing him something, what looks like little boxes with something inside them, but he can't see what. They parade it before him like it is their booty, as if wanting to make him jealous or to prove that they have something of his. He can't see what it is, but he would swear it is what the girl has swiped from inside, something she got from some warehouse or office or other. He laughs as he watches the kids running alongside the convoy. He laughs because they are laughing at him, sitting on the reels of copper thread, because in the end he did not catch the girl. Who knows what she got? Probably things without importance, he would never know.

They are the kids from the encampments, from the gypsy shacks; the kids from the ruins and the caravans where their parents and uncles and aunts are scraping by...Who knows who they live with? They run on the other side of the fence, under the motorway junctions and slip roads; they run at the speed of the train. There are lots of them and they keep passing the flags between them. There is one who he can hear shouting because he has a limp and is dragging his leg behind him. He cannot keep up. Another two are on bikes... He could have been one of them, one of the ones asking him what he's doing up there, shouting as loud as they can... He could have been one of them. He sees the men coming out of the huts and shacks between the waste ground and the reed beds around the tracks. They shout at the kids who are shouting at him. Anyone could have got in, Dexeus thinks to himself, as he spies the sea in the distance, the calm sea.

Guardians of Contemporary Art

Jordi Puntí

Translated from Catalan by
Maruxa Relaño & Martha Tennent

I REMEMBER MY PHONE vibrating in my trouser pocket and seeing Regina's name on the screen.

'What?' I answered in a low voice. I skipped the formalities because we weren't allowed to use our phones inside the museum. And besides, I'd been letting her stay with me for the last three weeks, as a favour, and we saw each other every day. We were practically sisters then.

'You sitting down?' she said. 'I've found a place.'

'No way.'

'Yep, I've rented a ground floor apartment. Dirt cheap and super cute, tia.'

'A ground floor? Where?'

'El Carmel.'

'El Carmel?' I blurted out in a whisper, trying to stifle my surprise.

'That's right. Carrer de la Murtra.'

'Don't you think that's a bit far, Regina? It's a long way away.'

'Nope. I'll tell you about it tonight.'

I wanted to press her on the matter, to forestall the trouble I saw looming ahead, the disaster that was brewing, but, in her excitement, she'd already hung up.

Regina and I met four years ago at the MACBA, the

Museum of Contemporary Art in Barcelona, where we work as guards. We get along because we're the same age, both with thwarted careers as young entrepreneurs. She wanted to start a cupcake and brownie business for children's parties, but she failed because mums always insist on showing other mums that they know how to make their own cupcakes and brownies. And me, I spent my savings and my time designing an app that turned guided museum tours into comedy monologues that people could follow with a headset, but the directors were terrified at the prospect of visitors succumbing to hilarity in front of a Tàpies or a Miró.

We can't talk much during the day, because as guards we're constantly changing rooms, even floors, but our schedules at MACBA often coincide and Regina and I can have lunch together. When the weather's nice we sit on the wall in Plaça dels Àngels in our uniforms, munching on Tupperware salads while we gossip about co-workers until the clack-clacking of the skateboarders starts to get on our nerves. Then we seek refuge in L'Horiginal and have a coffee before resuming our posts as guardians of contemporary art.

There's a prevalent myth according to which guards at museums and art galleries are frustrated artists atoning for a lack of talent by their many hours of contemplating the work of the masters. In the case of Regina and me, this scenario can't be ruled out, and that's why I'd like to chronicle our little adventure, though I much prefer the cliché that all Hollywood waiters are actors hoping for a breakout role, or even the one about ball kids at a tennis match, one metre away from their dream, awaiting the errors of those who succeed.

The truth of the matter is that working at MACBA, supervising visitors with amazed or ecstatic faces as they stand before works that perhaps not even the artists understood, is not a lifelong dream of ours. But it offers a salary, and it does provide an inside view of the circus show that is the art scene, even if it's through drudgery and routine. Besides, the daily interaction with the works sharpens our taste, it helps us understand what we like and what bores us. We try not to judge anything at first glance, but guarding Christian Boltanski's 'Reserve of Dead Swiss', with all those metal boxes stacked up to impress you and make you claustrophobic, isn't exactly the same as pondering what Juan Muñoz's sculptures of smiling Chinese people are trying to convey. Nor does time pass as quickly when forced to endure three hours of one of Gordon Matta-Clark's weird, looped videos as it does when entertained by visitors' surprised faces as they come upon the extravagances of Carlos Pazos. Then there's the surprise element of our more spontaneous guests, which always catches you napping. The man who thought to masturbate before a poster of the Guerrilla Girls. The blind guy who needed to feel a sculpture by Susana Solano. The grandmother who turns up once a month to claim a piece by Torres-Garcia that the Nationalists apparently stole from her family during the Civil War. And if you happen to be scheduled to work on the weekend, you have those Sunday mornings which are *so exhausting*, with kids running amok and getting lost from one room to another, or attempting to dismantle Marcel Broodthaers's installation in front of their adoring parents, or weeping at lunchtime, completely spent. We share this world, Regina and I, we endure it and mock it together, and that's how we've become close.

Maybe I should point out that Regina had started crashing on my couch, a temporary arrangement, after she broke up with her boyfriend. We never talked about the length of her stay, but I wasn't worried. I knew she was driven, had initiative, and wouldn't allow things to sour. Plus, she was tired of moving from place to place, and looked forward to being on her own. Less than six months had passed since she'd left her umpteenth apartment share to live with some kind of conceptual artist she'd met precisely at MACBA. He said he was an artist, but he had no work to speak of, just a bunch of ideas in his head, impracticable projects that required a budget he didn't have, nor ever would.

Regina met him one morning when he was on a guided tour. The guy, who went by the artistic name of El Burla – The Mocker – was pretty unprepossessing. To make ends meet, he earned a few euros from a community centre by accompanying a group of elderly people who were taking a course on current trends in the art world. During a pause, while the senescents contemplated Joan Brossa's object-poems, he approached Regina, who was guarding the room that day.

'Are you also a work of art?' he said with a studied smile.

'Moron…' she deadpanned, without even glancing at him or moving a facial muscle, and when he was about to leave, she added: 'Of course I'm a work of art. This *is* a museum, isn't it?'

Despite the lame opener, Regina told me she sensed a connection right away. I suspect they didn't fall in love or anything, and it was all just a tacit, non-verbal agreement disguised as mutual attraction. The sexual urge was there, of course, and the first few weeks Regina came to work looking like she'd had little sleep, with a happy grin that filled me with envy. We communicated mainly through emojis when we texted from room to room, and in the morning I'd send her a sleepy face with a bunch of Zzzs, or the one with sunglasses, and she'd respond with an explosion of firecrackers, gymnasts, tongues, hearts, bottles of champagne and even, once, a chocolate-glazed donut.

After the fever pitch subsided, however, it became clear that we'd connected for reasons that were both personal and divergent. Regina had found the perfect excuse to leave her shared apartment and take one step further into adulthood, which is to say into the privilege of not having to remember which refrigerator shelf was hers. Then there was the fact that, in those last few months, she'd grown increasingly annoyed by her roommates: a militant vegan couple who ate only raw vegetables and had a sour body odour of fermented garlic, plus a Chilean singer-songwriter who spent his days in a smoked-up haze, rehearsing songs of unrequited love. A lethal combination.

It was soon plain that the guy, El Burla, I mean, had fallen for Regina for artistic reasons. After they'd been together for two months, living in a fifth-floor walkup – a minuscule chambre de bonne he called a loft – he suggested that she take part in a new project of his, one of those he meticulously outlined in his black Moleskine notebook. The idea was for Regina to produce a list of ex-boyfriends, understood in the broadest sense of the word. They included the boy she played doctor with when she was eight, the pimple-faced teen who first kissed her, and the friend of a friend she made out with on the beach one night and never again. She just needed to remember their names. El Burla would find them wherever they were, all these years later, and in an updated version of courtly love, he'd confront them, challenge them to defend his Queen's honour. Then, continuing with the provocation, he would allow himself to be roughed up and mistreated by her former lovers. The finished work that would one day be displayed, maybe even at MACBA, would consist of the photos and videos of the bruises, blows, cuts and scars that would cover his body, all of them incurred in her name. 'Reina Regina'. 'Queen Regina', the work would be called.

Regina played along from the start, although she had her reservations. The idea of being a contemporary artist's muse was flattering, but the possibility of stirring up her past terrified her. When she told me about it, I tried to advise her without being overbearing. I cautioned her that bohemian life is grand in biographies of dead artists, but no one ever thinks about the suffering endured while they're alive. In the end, after mulling it over a few days, Regina decided to give him a chance. She handed El Burla a list of eight names of old boyfriends and guys she'd had flings with; she even tried to remember details that might prove helpful: when and where she'd met them, if the relationship was short or long-term, painful or memorable, if they had sex rarely or often.

He started tracking them down, trawling through Facebook and Instagram, and, to use clickbait lingo, *you won't believe what happened next.* As he collected data and jotted it down in his notebook, El Burla grew jealous. The roster of guys became his rivals from the past. He tried to discover what they were doing now, and with the blasé attitude of a private eye, he showed Regina recent photos of them. She would never have renewed contact with those shadowy memories, but her vivacious, playful curiosity, rather than encourage the budding artist, crushed him, made him suspicious and unsettled. She noticed and tried to comfort him, to no avail. The day El Burla, slit-eyed and tortured by jealousy, suggested she'd been a bit of a slut, with such a long list of men in her past, Regina packed up her things and left him alone in his miserable loft.

'You'll never amount to anything, you phoney,' she said.

The ground floor apartment, which Regina finally rented despite my misgivings, was on Carrer de la Murtra, in El Carmel. It was one of those quiet streets with a steep incline, one side seeming to end at the rocky edge of the mountain, the other offering views of a far-off sliver of sea, merging with the blue of the Barcelona sky.

'It's very close to the subway stop,' she told me as she showed me the apartment, 'and in no time, mark my words, all this will be gentrified. Yesterday I went for a stroll around the neighbourhood, and a little further along, on Carrer Lugo, I discovered a yoga studio and a flower shop run by a French girl. And down the street, there's a tattoo parlour and a bar called *El Rincón de Zamora* – *molt autèntic.* On Sunday mornings they even serve churros. One write-up in *Time Out* and you'll see, everybody's moving up here.'

'Always the groundbreaker...'

I didn't want to disappoint her, you understand. I gave an enthusiastic *sí* to everything: it was what she needed. To live alone and forget that two-bit artist, even if it meant moving into a small, dark apartment an hour's subway ride from work. The ground floor was part of a four-story building, and you entered straight off the street, then through a door at the end of a narrow corridor from which a flight of stairs led up to the other floors. In front of her door was a small vestibule that reeked of bleach, with a few post-war mailboxes, a plastic bin for discarded commercial mail, and a cupboard for the electricity and water meters. The light on the stairs was automatic and made a metallic click when it turned on and off.

When I entered her apartment, it seemed so dark and gloomy I was surprised it wasn't in fact the portal to a mineshaft that burrowed into the mountain. The door opened to an unpretentious entryway: read *tiny*. The former tenant had left behind a sun-shaped mirror and a low shelf with a pile of *Selecciones del Reader's Digest*, a magazine of translated articles. To the left was a large enough room, as yet unfurnished, with a window onto the street, and next to it a bedroom that could barely hold a double bed, French size, and a nightstand. Maybe because it was November and sunny, the afternoon light streamed through the windows quite brazenly. Regina said she might put up curtains, for privacy, but she never did. Down the hall to the right, at the other end of the apartment, was a bathroom with a shower, and a kitchen that led to a narrow, dark inner court with a corner for the washing machine and a few dusty clotheslines. A greenish plastic roof, meant to protect laundry from the rain, ate up what little sunlight might have entered, submerging everything in thick penumbra, as if you were in the heart of hearts of a tropical jungle, about to witness

Colonel Kurtz's spasms as he utters his final words: *The horror! The horror!*

With this scenario, you might have expected Regina to be down in the dumps, but it was just the opposite. I mentioned earlier that she was driven, but maybe I should have said impulsive, which is not exactly the same. Impulse often bypasses the reflection needed to avoid trouble and second-guessing. In her case, however, her impetuous decisions were justified by a desire 'to experiment, to expose myself to the unfamiliar, to explore the mysteries of existence' (her words). I'll explain.

That first afternoon, as we were leaving her place, Regina asked me to read the names on the mailboxes. There were four, in addition to her own, meaning there was only one apartment per floor. For some reason they were all unusual names, let's put it that way. Daniel Mackintosh. The Petrarca family, 'Italians,' she said. Juan, Juana, and Juanet Burrull. And on the top floor, the initials P. M. B. I read them all out loud, with an intonation somewhere between amused and incredulous, because that's what she expected.

'Right?' she said, opening her hands and questioning me with wide eyes. 'Hard to beat. With neighbours like that, and the chance to discover what life is like on the ground floor, now you understand why I had to rent this, no?'

I forced myself to utter a compelling *sí*, and at this point, I should say that I feel partly responsible for her renewed zest, and what happened later; perhaps that's why I'm dwelling on the details here, trying to shake off my remorse. Although the break-up with the artist formerly known as El Burla hadn't been dramatic, leaving her home, however precarious it may have been, and having to sleep on my couch, shower with my shampoo, and plod around in slippers in a place that wasn't her own, was making her more and more miserable. Half an hour before the end of our workday at the museum, I'd send her an emoji of a clock and a smiley face, and she'd respond reluctantly, ten minutes later, with the image of a spider web.

I had to come up with something to distract Regina. So, one Sunday, a week after she'd moved in, I convinced her to go to the cinematheque. They were screening a retrospective of Werner Herzog documentaries, and *Encounters at the End of the World* was showing that afternoon. It came strongly recommended by a curator at the museum, who enjoyed chatting to room guards because it made her feel less elitist. I'd seen the delirious *Fitzcarraldo* many years ago, but to Regina, Herzog was an unknown film director. The stories of all those people trying to live a normal life in Antarctica, in the most extreme weather conditions, amazed her. You might say she had some sort of epiphany, and filled with awe, she asked to stay for the next show, *Grizzly Man*. From then on, she tried to see all the documentaries in the retrospective, from *Wings of Hope* to *Cave of Forgotten Dreams*, which she declared a masterpiece. She'd go in without knowing what the film was about, only that Werner Herzog was the director, and when she arrived home at night, she'd describe it to me with a sort of transcendent excitement.

'He's an incredible director, Lola,' she'd say, 'but what truly blows me away is his voice. He speaks English with that German accent, which can be harsh and comical at the same time, but then his tone is so gentle when he asks a difficult question or describes such extraordinary things… Sometimes I think it's thanks to that voice of his that things happen. As if he *made* them happen, or rather, as if the world existed just so he could explore it, describe it with images. Maybe that's how we should all live, waiting for Werner Herzog to discover us and turn us into a character in a documentary.'

Energised by this new mood, the next day she started searching the internet for an apartment.

Once the lease was signed, Regina bought some second-hand furniture, and as it was a small apartment, right away she had it all set up. I drove her there and helped her move her boxes and suitcases the day she left. We toasted with champagne to celebrate, and I asked if she'd throw a house-warming party for her friends.

'I haven't decided,' she said. 'Sometimes I think this should be my secret place in the world, and no one needs to know exactly where I live. No one but you, of course, and my new neighbours. At the moment I think I want a cat to keep me company...' and she smiled so confidently it was disturbing.

As the weeks passed, the mood inspired in her by Werner Herzog settled, quite naturally, into every corner of the ground floor apartment, and who knows if eventually it dissipated just as naturally. I hadn't been back to her place, but when we had lunch together, she'd describe the latest developments with an air of exceptionality that seemed, at times, to be dictated by an alien inner voice: Herzog's slightly lisping voice, imagine that!

'One day, Lola, you realise that the hours spent in a ground floor apartment are a rite of passage between public and private life,' she told me as we shared a joint after lunch. 'Like a secret corridor leading to one's innermost domain. Only the façade separates us, and this very close coexistence is both a privilege and a calamity that must be accepted. When my windows are open and the light streams in, life also enters, and you learn that your daily horizon is other people, all those busts and torsos that walk by like urban centaurs. And then there's the fact that, in a ground floor apartment, you sense beneath you the heartbeat of the earth, the subsoil that awaits us patiently until the day we return to it. It's no surprise I should feel a bond stretching back centuries, connecting me to my ancestors, as if I, too, were alone in my cave, warming myself by the primaeval fire of the gods...'

(I could mention that her apartment had central heating, but that's neither here nor there.)

Meanwhile, just as I'd expected, the prosaic counterpoint to all this frenzy was offered by the neighbours in the building. Little by little, Regina would come to know all but one of them, the person on the top floor, and had faces to match the voices she heard from behind her door. She spoke to me affectionately about this, but I noticed in her voice a touch of condescension, if not disappointment, as if they hadn't lived up to her expectations.

The neighbour on the first floor, Daniel Mackintosh, was an Argentine who worked as a cook in a pizzeria in Vallcarca. One afternoon, he knocked on Regina's door, wanting to collect a striped T-shirt that had fallen onto her back patio – he played rugby with friends on Thursday evenings – and she broke the ice by asking about his last name. He told her about his Scottish great-grandfather, who emigrated from Edinburgh to Buenos Aires a hundred years ago to work on the construction of the railway line. My friend immediately perked up, but when she expressed interest in learning more (as Herzog would have), the young man showed his true colours: he grew surly and monosyllabic, and soon found an excuse to say goodbye.

Behind the Petrarca Family from the mailbox, there was only a widowed lady on the second floor, correctly baptised as Laura, over ninety years old and no doubt with a story to tell. Her memory, however, was either scant or entirely lost in the shrunken labyrinths of her mind, and she was cared for by a stern Polish woman who acted as a firewall, isolating her even more from the world. Regina had only seen her neighbour once, the afternoon she knocked on her door to introduce herself. The little old lady had looked like a sweet, wrinkled raisin sitting in her armchair, scrutinising Regina with green eyes so vivid it seemed they were sending SOS signals every time she blinked. But the Polish woman had announced it was time for her umpteenth pill and invited Regina to leave.

The Burrulls on the third floor could pass for a family of circus artists, all of them with thin, elongated faces like actors in a vertically stretched Cinemascope, but their uniqueness was exhausted in the statement on the mailbox. Juan, Juana, and Juanet were precisely that: three Juans made from the same mould. Nothing more. The father and the mother didn't look like a couple at all, more like twins, and their six-year-old was a male mini-me of both of them. They offered scant interest, but Regina got along with them out of necessity, thanks primarily to Juanet, who would run down the stairs and rap on her door asking for candy as if her apartment were a shop.

Those brief encounters helped her obtain information, and through The Juans – she summed them up as a collective – she learned something about the woman who lived on the top floor. She was elusive, about fifty years old, more a nighthawk than a day person. No one knew her line of work, she wouldn't appear for weeks on end (away on a trip perhaps?), and occasionally she received an American magazine, *Artforum,* that wouldn't fit in the mailbox. And her initials: what name did they conceal? But wait, *no*, those belonged to the former tenant; the current one hadn't even bothered to change them. By the way, it was a good thing that the previous tenant, Patrícia *Morticia*, as The Juans called her, had left, because for years she'd made life impossible for her neighbours: loud music, a penchant for breeding snakes at home, nocturnal meetings of ufologists on her terrace trying to make contact with the outer rim…

In a nutshell, after a few weeks, and to maintain the momentum around her 'life experiment on the ground floor' (her words, it should be noted), Regina turned her attention to the intrigues surrounding the neighbour on the top floor. All the clues indicated she was an artist, but what kind? Conceptual, surreal, digital, algorithmic? Twice a week, always at different times, Regina went up to her apartment and rang the doorbell, but no one ever answered. Once she even dared to look under the mat; if she'd found a key there, I know she would have used it. If there was a noise in the hallway while she was at home, she rushed to wrench open the door. But she always encountered the vertically moronic smirk of The Juans ('I want candy!'), or the grim countenance of the Polish carer, or the back of Mackintosh Man, who fled, pretending not to hear her.

'Sometimes, Lola, I feel I'm being treated like the building doorman,' she'd vent. 'And I'm the opposite of that. They still haven't figured it out. If I want to keep an eye on people, I have my work here at MACBA.'

'Of course,' I would agree, with what I must admit was false deference. 'Up in El Carmel they've got everything backwards, estimada. *You* are the work of art people should go and see. You're way too cool for that neighbourhood, a luxury item. They don't deserve you.'

'Exactly.'

Although it was just an inconsequential comment, small talk really, some of my words must have stuck. Regina's like that, you never know what she'll do next. The point is, when the weather turned good in summer, her whole routine intensified. If she was home, going about her chores or just sitting in the armchair with the computer on her lap, she'd open the windows so the casual sounds of the street spilled into the apartment. She liked to hear the happy cries of children playing a few houses away, a mother's song as she pushed her baby in her stroller, a couple's heated argument... The way she explained it, any novelty transported her, for no particular reason other than she was so inclined.

'Now I know why I don't need curtains,' she'd say. 'It's like living in Scandinavia, I don't lower the blinds until I go to sleep. Every now and then an anonymous pedestrian walks by my window and can't resist the urge to peep inside. And I'm ready to welcome the sideways glances, whether they're shy, furtive, or penetrating. I sense them and look up at the right time, and the truth is they keep me company, as if they were dressing me instead of undressing me.'

It was hot and Regina went around the house barefoot, wearing shorts and a tank top; the more prudish among her neighbours must have found it excessive, almost indecent, but she didn't notice. It's like this: while she waited for the artist on the top floor to show signs of life, Regina, through some unconscious desire for connection, was turning herself into a showcase of contemporary life, an art project in plain view of everyone.

Plus, now she had a cat. His name was Werner, of course, and true to his namesake, he often jumped out of the window to explore the neighbourhood. If he was gone a while, Regina headed up the street barefoot looking for him, calling his name, and every now and then a curious neighbour would stop and engage her in conversation for a few minutes. She almost never found Werner, but when she returned he'd be asleep in the entrance hall, atop a stack of *Selecciones*.

At night, she told me, she'd lower the blinds some but leave her window open so the air would circulate, and fall asleep in bed, lulled by the latent murmurs of the street. That part of El Carmel was quiet in the early morning, it didn't seem like a city at all. The roar of a motorcycle, the puff of a smoker's cigarette, the wayward footsteps of a straggler, would infiltrate her dreams, and the next day she awoke with an agitation of the soul that was unfamiliar, and, to her, invigorating.

She'd come to work at the museum looking relaxed, as if by entering MACBA she had crossed to the other side of the mirror and, focused on her job as guardian of contemporary art, she became invisible. All the same, for reasons I can't fully explain, I was uncomfortable with her thing about the ghost artist upstairs, which was rapidly becoming an obsession. Ever vigilant, now it was Regina who collected the *Artforum* issues for her neighbour; she hurried to yank them from the mailbox before The Juans could disturb them. From the magazine subscription, she learned they were addressed to Laughing Out Loud, or LOL, and she wondered if there was a company behind it, an organisation. Perhaps it was the name the mysterious woman went by in the art scene. When she googled the phrase, however, she got millions of hits, including a couple of art galleries in the United States and Australia, and it was impossible to discover anything. The flood of useless information was bewildering, and Regina obsessed, sensing a dead end from which she might never emerge.

'What if it turns out that. . .?'

More and more, her sentences began with this refrain, and she'd indulge her bizarre theories about the artist. Months went by and nothing changed, and I confess I couldn't stand it much longer. One October evening, when Regina had been in the ground floor apartment almost a year, I decided to pay her a surprise visit and try to clarify some things. As I walked towards her place, Carrer de la Murtra was submerged in silence. The first cold spell had arrived, and everyone sheltered inside their homes for dinner. When I reached her apartment, instead of ringing the doorbell I sneaked up to the living room window and peered inside. With the shutter completely raised, it looked more like a shop window, and the iron grille patterned the scene like a jigsaw puzzle. It occurred to me that, by way of greeting, I'd tap on the window and do my best monster impression, give her a fright. But Regina wasn't there. *She's probably in the kitchen or bathroom,* I thought. The floor lamp gave the living room a warm glow, conferring an evanescent patina of age on its contents, the wicker chair, the pot with the cyclamen I'd given her, the laptop on the coffee table, which seemed distorted by a darkness that now, seen from the outside, appeared to emanate from the ceiling, about to engulf everything. Suddenly Regina entered the frame, and I instinctively withdrew into the shadows. It had been too long and my joke had deflated. Now I might actually scare her. Regina stretched out on the couch and I noticed she was talking to herself, but I couldn't understand what she was saying. After a while, she closed her eyes and seemed to be praying, or rather reciting a poem from memory. Half a minute passed, maybe more, and the scene was imbued with a mysticism that made me feel like a foolish gumshoe. I was about to leave without saying anything when the stairwell light came on. I crossed to the other side of the street so as not to draw attention and saw Regina rise and go to the door. She must have heard the light clicking on, or the footsteps of a neighbour coming down the stairs. Then she did a strange thing: she rested her cheek against the door, as if to caress the figure that crept down the hall. She stood there for a few seconds. From my hiding place, I watched the street door open. Regina's face appeared in the window, trying to catch a glimpse of the person who was leaving, seizing a new opportunity to unmask that stupid woman from the top-floor apartment. But alas, it wasn't to be. Daniel Mackintosh exited, bundled in an anorak and wearing a baseball cap, and with quick steps he strode up the sidewalk. Realising the person had headed away in the opposite direction, Regina pressed her forehead, nose and lips against the windowpane, and her features distorted into an amused childish grimace. I burst out laughing, transfixed, frightened, and for a moment I was sure she'd seen me standing there like a statue. But no, she had not.

Wrapped in her thoughts, she returned to the couch, and I made my way to the subway. From the platform, while I waited for the train, I sent her emojis of a full moon and a steaming cup of tea. I put my phone away without waiting for a reply. I didn't know how to tell her it's me. The so-called artist on the top floor is me.

Atoms Like Snowflakes

Carlota Gurt

Translated from the Catalan by Mary Ann Newman

WE ARE IN A CITY where all the streets go up and down, urbanism on an inclined plane, the goddamned omnipresent sea or mountains, sea to the south, mountains to the north, and a scar in the form of an avenue that bisects the city on the diagonal – skewed along a physical, moral, class angle that is its scourge – and the hills that try helplessly to constrain it so it doesn't overflow in all directions. We are in an uncontainable city.

Yes, Senyora P. lives in Barcelona, and right now she is walking up a street – a torrent, as they call it, in this case a torrent of flowers, à la Rodoreda. But there are no longer any fragrant camellias or wisteria to be seen, now it's all rows of motorcycles and the pestilent hydrography painted on the pavement by dog piss. She is sweating unbearably, not just because of the Via Crucis of the steep incline, but also because she is dragging her shopping cart behind her, from which a bulky rectangular package sticks out two hands high, containing a device which, despite its laughable weight of a mere three kilos and 300 grams, is capable of executing a thorny task, surely the thorniest task there is, a task which no human being wishes to carry out.

The clerk had offered her free home delivery but that would have meant waiting until the next day, and Senyora P.

has had enough. She has been saving up, and dreaming and, above all, waiting, for ten years.

She drags the shopping cart up the last few metres to the door. Huffing and puffing, she crosses the vestibule and casts one more glance at the lair of the concierge, which has stood empty for decades. In this new century, concierges are relics only lavished on the posh menagerie of the Upper Diagonal.

She likes living on the ground floor, at street level. It seems less ambitious and more human to her than being caged in a sixth-floor apartment with too much light to stay grounded. In the foyer, she catches a glimpse of herself in the mirror. *Marymotherofgod*, if she doesn't look like a crazy old woman, in her housecoat, with a mop of white hair rebelling like a raging storm at sea. She needs to go to the hairdresser's, but since her lifelong salon went out of business, the time has never seemed right to try one of those spectacular modern establishments, nor does she have any reason to. To be honest, why would she?

A rather unsubtle moustache marks her upper lip which, in turn, shrinks back inside her mouth, leaving no doubt that today, yet again, she is not wearing her teeth. Lately, she just doesn't put them in, she doesn't see the point and, what's more, she's a bit afraid she'll glue them in with the denture adhesive and never be able to take them out again. Sometimes she even dreams about it. She sees Senyor P. approaching her with a hammer and chisel to yank the fake smile out of her gums. Maybe, in fact, this is the thing: she has never tolerated dishonesty or trying to gussy up ugliness. That must be why she lives in this city, though we could certainly find someone who would say exactly the opposite.

Once in the living room, she doesn't stop to rest for so much as a minute. She takes the unwieldy package out of the cart and unwraps it impatiently. Ten years of waiting and now, finally, the eraser is on the table. Luckily, she still has a head for technological things. Once she's read the short manual, she plugs in the machine and the main funnel begins to emit a relaxing buzz.

She places the pinky toe of her left foot inside it and feels a delightful tingling, a melodic wave that flows over her skin. At the other end of the funnel, a little cloud is coming out that soon dissolves into the air: her invaluable contribution to the most polluted air in Europe.

The shopkeeper was right, it didn't hurt a bit. That was the only thing that had given her pause, the pain. Well, the pain and the blood, but there isn't so much as a drop. Once she has carried out the deatomisation test, she pulls her foot back, sans small toe, and sticks the exhaust duct out the window. Everything's ready.

Before starting the procedure, she goes to the kitchen, picks up two bars of dark chocolate and leans on the windowsill to contemplate the bustle of the city for the last time. She lets the chocolate melt in her mouth. It's delivery time: vans with four blinking lights and drivers quick to honk. The walls, like everything else, are obliterated under the young people's uninspired graffiti, as if by plastering a twisted signature there they were taking possession of something. They, the dispossessed, it's the only way for them to own anything. But today Senyora P. is not grumbling, she even looks at the tags with magnanimity and is amused to think that, before she goes, she too might leave her signature on the façade of the building where she has spent her entire life, a good life.

The indifference on the faces of the passersby surprises her. It's out of sync with the joy she is feeling. She wished everyone was singing and dancing as if in a musical, and passing trucks were tossing out candy, and everyone was having canelons for lunch. Her day of liberation is here.

But no. Ever since some scoundrel put canelons in a different kind of eraser nurtured over decades that also turns everything into smoke, the cannelloni brought here by fin-de-siècle Italian chefs have lost all interest; old-fashioned cooking is out of fashion.

She leaves the window half-open and ensconces herself on the sofa with the still-buzzing machine in front of her. The instructions make it clear that you must proceed from the feet to the head so as not to leave the job half-done.

She sticks her whole left foot inside, all at once, ignoring the explicit warning to proceed bit by bit to avert obstructions. The eraser lets out a howl and Senyora P. fears the worst, but the contraption starts to deatomise her foot. She feels her molecules being decomposed with a caress.

Her foot is erased, but not the memory of when she broke it a year ago and her son had to come and live with her for a few weeks. Manel. Poor Manel, he's not going to understand. Is it so hard to see that she's done all she's going to do? That she has no reason to keep getting up in the morning?

Manel insists that she's depressed. He doesn't get it. Even as a kid he was a little peculiar, in his own world, playing with his strings and gadgets. He's not a bad kid, but he lives in his own bubble. He always takes her by the hand, imitating gestures he's seen. He can't find his own way to express what he's feeling. Or maybe he doesn't feel anything. Manel and feelings, a fish on a bicycle.

She sticks her whole leg into the funnel, little by little now, so as not to overwhelm the machine. When the tickling is almost at her groin the phone rings. Damn, she forgot to disconnect it. She tries to ignore it. It rings ten times and stops. Finally. But it starts up again right away.

She gets up, a little aggravated, balancing on the foot she still has and holding on to the shelves full of books from fifty years ago that no one has ever read. Her knee creaks, the office door creaks, the city of last century also creaks under the pressure of the new city pulverising it. She makes her way down the hall to the telephone, which is now ringing for the third time.

'Yes? Manel, I can't talk now. No, you don't need to come over, I have things to do. What things? Things I want to do, son, that's all. But take care. You know I won't be around much longer. No, I'm fine, just fine. Big kiss. I love you. No, don't be stubborn, there's nothing wrong, can't I even say I love you? Yes, okay, talk later.'

She unplugs the phone and the creaking starts again, the creaking that precedes the final collapse.

When she gets back to the sofa, she's exhausted from the expedition. She'd better get a move on. It's time for the right leg. She resists the temptation to stick it in all at once and get it over with, and decides to enjoy the pleasure of the moment. That's it, no more walking, no more varicose veins – those blue worms that tunnel down her legs – no more cramps, no more torture of climbing stairs. Outside, the exhaust tube excretes a thick cloud of smoke.

The eraser starts to make a blur of her pubis and for a moment, like a sleeping beauty after a hundred years of lethargy, her strawberry wakes up – that's what Senyor P. used to call it when he played with it – and all those nights of naughty secrets with her husband rush into her head, and the moment when he lost his drive, and she wasn't in the mood anymore and they would just cuddle tenderly, more out of habit than love. Or maybe not, maybe that's exactly what love is, she doesn't know anymore. She surrenders to thinking about the nature of love and remembering that immense and fleeting sensation. Love, the antithesis of the eraser: a machine that creates matter where there was none. Without her even realising it, the funnel has sucked up her belly button.

Outside she hears two women's voices talking about incomprehensible things in that hellish language that's spreading through every neighbourhood like a plague. She's doing the right thing to leave now, just in time, before the city becomes entirely unintelligible to her, leaving now, happy and in full possession of her faculties, cushioned by the sweet memories of the seven-and-a-half decades that she has been beating this asphalt. When you're playing cards, you also have to know how to stand with a seven-and-a-half to win.

Now she wonders if she should lift her arms and leave them for the end or stick them into the machine. She doesn't have enough stomach muscles left to get up and consult the manual or stop the eraser and think about it for a while. *Zumzum.* Time to decide. Tick-tock.

With the wisdom of Solomon, she decides to stick one arm in and leave the other for the end. Her right hand sinks into the funnel. Goodbye pain in her joints every time she opens a can of tuna, opens the blinds, closes the gas valve. Goodbye writing with a shaky pulse. Goodbye holding Manel's limp hand, always sweaty and ridiculously fearful, having to sense his attempts at tenderness.

What a relief!

The contraption moves up past her withered nipples and swallows the parchment skin of her breasts, the same breasts she used to parade through the streets of Gràcia during the Festa Major, the August street festival that has morphed into an absurd mess of beer, tourists, and gigantic amplifiers; the same breasts that in her youth coveted a full life and discovered the enigmas of maternity; the breasts that fed Manel when he was born, which as a baby he had already suckled with the same scant desire with which he now imbibed life.

The atoms of her heart are already dissolving out through the exhaust pipe, and Senyora P. feels a comforting inner silence. Enough boom-boom. Infinite serenity. She wishes she could thrust herself in so the eraser could swallow her up in one gulp, but she restrains herself. Now all that is left is her head and her left arm, which is resting on her nest of hair.

She feels the turbulent massage of the extractor at her chin and, before it's too late, she decides to hear her own voice for the last time and shouts the first thing that comes into her head, not trying to say anything brilliant, because she doesn't have time to think. She just bursts out with all her lung power, *I'm on my waaay*, but she hasn't even got so far as the 'y' when the eraser silences her on its determined way to her nose and ears.

Senyora P. isn't focusing on odours — she hasn't smelled anything in years — but on sounds. She hears her upstairs neighbour beating an egg, a truck wheezing to reach the top of the hill, the back and forth of a pair of high heels punishing the sidewalk and, in the background, the hypnotic buzz of the eraser. Suddenly, total silence with the density of lava, which is a little intimidating and, more than anything, out of character for this uncontainable city, always screeching like a starving newborn.

Her eyes open wide as she notices the tickling at her cheeks. She looks at the ceiling and the light fixture that Senyor P. bought too many years ago in that store that doesn't exist anymore. Remembering this, the liberating joy she feels is tinged with an old sadness. Her eyes become moist and there is still enough time for them to squeeze out one last tear which, like her tired pupils, soon turns to atoms.

The funnel chews up her parietal and frontal lobes, and she is assaulted by an uncontrolled army of memories bubbling up amid disconnected sensations. Her memory is dissolving like an effervescent tablet. Fragile, ephemeral bubbles. Memory in eruption.

The taste of horseradish as the breeze ran through her hair on the green tricycle. The warm smell of madeleines as she felt Senyor P.'s hands on her waist. A velvety sensation and her mother's fava beans à la catalana. A strange iron aftertaste as she sees herself walking down the Portal de l'Àngel holding Manel by the hand. The acidic impression of her first French class with Mlle Thibaut in that neighbourhood of houses clustered on the hill, leery of the city at their feet. A restful hum as she watched her father loading sacks of flour. A spongy warmth as Manel recited the Christmas poem like an automaton. The salty vertigo of the night she lost her virginity. The strident bitterness of the day she cut herself on the knife for carving ham off the bone. The rough sketches she traced with her footsteps on the Barcelona of yore, now dead. The fossilised memories pile up without allowing her time to react, and soon the eraser vacuums up her language and she can no longer sensibly articulate ideas.

Everything turns into sensation, thought in its pure state.

Without hearing or sight, she can't perceive how close her son is, how a few seconds ago he turned the southern corner and, seeing the thick smoke pouring from the ground-floor window, started running at full speed.

He stops in surprise when he reaches the smoke, as it doesn't smell of burning. He sniffs it with a scientific curiosity and breathes in a few very tiny air bubbles that make him sneeze. For a moment he feels a mass of sensations: a strident bitterness, a spongy warmth, a salty vertigo and, above all, a total freedom, a science fiction plenitude. He dispels these indecipherable emotions, pulling the curtains aside in one fell swoop and watching his mother's last hairs disappearing into the funnel. He jumps over the window bar and rushes to turn off the machine.

He gets there just in time to avert her complete volatilisation. Her left hand, which had been resting on her head, has been salvaged. He will keep it in a fishbowl full of formaldehyde at 36.5 degrees Celsius. Every morning he will hold that warm piece of dead flesh just as he has always done, and with the obstinacy of a man who can't tolerate things moving forward, changing and dying, he will persist in not understanding why his mother wanted to disappear.

To no avail, though, because the rest of Senyora P. is drifting freely down the street, like a liberating torrent of atoms sneaking into all kinds of noses, invading Greek and Roman protuberances, climbing clandestinely into nasal cavities like an invisible neurotoxin, a chemical weapon insisting on spreading happiness amid all the urban din. Her molecules are now inseparable from those of the conquered organisms, irreversibly amalgamated with them.

Maybe this, too, is the city, the promiscuity of atoms that fall lightly onto the asphalt like flakes of snow, burying the times and the ruins of past lives.

This evening, in ancient Barcino, where all the streets go up and down, someone will eat a plate of canelons with delight.

Every Colour

Marta Orriols

Translated from the Catalan by Julia Sanches

THE TWO PLANES' WHITE contrails draw a soft x in the blue winter sky and, just like that, map out a remarkable coincidence.

The woman, though, is staring idly at the rooftops of Gràcia, where she loves to lose herself in thought whenever she's done hanging the laundry. She doesn't know what it is about them that's fascinated her all these years. They're a bit dirty, sure, but even their maze-like patchwork stirs up a comforting sense of freedom in Elena.

She has the urge to open the sketch pad she bought a couple of days ago and outline the rooftops she can see from where she stands. She'll draft it in charcoal first and then, if she finds the courage, she can move on to watercolour. She'll play with a selection of blacks and greys. She isn't in the right mindset for colour at the moment. This is her symbolic mourning for Bernat, for the last confused look he gave her from the doorway, and for the exhausted words that acted as a firebreak: 'I tried, Elena, I really tried.'

It was true. He had at least tried, while she'd done a confused dance to get out of a mortgage, dinner with the in-laws, an engagement, and also the fire and excitement of Bernat's body.

Elena picks up the basket and the bag of paintbrushes. Just as she's about to open the door, someone does the same from

83

the other side, and she finds herself face to face with a woman she's never seen before.

'Hey, sorry about that. Did I hurt you?' She has a steely voice and her black eyes study Elena with concern until she assures her that she's okay. 'Is there another clothesline lying around? I'm new to the building.'

'Over there. They're really old, though. Have you got much? I only hung up a handful of things, so you can use mine if you want. It's new.'

'Thanks, all I have is this uniform. I hope it dries fast! I'll need it for tomorrow.'

She stands on her tiptoes to reach the clothesline and Elena glimpses a flat, smooth belly, tanned skin and the perfect twirl of a belly button under her sweater. A knot in her stomach forces Elena to look down. They smile goodbye.

It's getting late. Elena still hasn't gotten used to the fact that she has a studio at home and doesn't need to go into the office anymore. Ever since Bernat left, time has either passed at a dangerous clip or slid by sadly. She puts her hair up in a bun and cracks open her new sketch pad. She obstinately sniffs the paper and runs her hand down the surface with the same soft touch a person might use on a lover's back, then starts drawing. On her desk is the organised chaos she so desperately needs: a metal box with tubes of oil paint, a tarnished palette, paintbrushes, scattered sketches, and an 'I Love New York' mug, stained with dribbles of colour.

She never said what her name was. She needs her uniform to dry by tomorrow. She pictures the woman dressed as a firefighter, a police officer, a security guard, a nurse. She shakes her head and focuses on the picture of the rooftops.

The next day she heads back upstairs to take down her clothes and finds a turquoise lace thong and a flight-attendant uniform next to her jeans. On the left breast pocket is the airline logo.

She can't help but check the size. The woman hadn't seemed particularly small, maybe because of her height, or her deep, throaty voice. At first, Elena is horrified by the turquoise thong – she can't stand certain colours – but then it starts fluttering pleasantly in the wind, and she is captivated. She unpegs all her clothes in one go and makes her way back home, irritated. She feels uneasy in a way that's hard to understand and quickly shies away from it. No one can match her when it comes to deflecting ambiguous thoughts, which is why it takes her no time at all to push back the sudden memory of the student she'd shared a flat with in Florence during Erasmus. To draw her nude, Elena had to make sure her gaze and the dexterity of her hand worked on a physical and intellectual level, because a naked body is more than just a body: it's also skeleton and skin, movement and flesh, sensuousness and demeanour. The point of the exercise was to capture the body from a purely artistic point of view, but Elena's uncurbed interest in the female form had distorted her perspective, which did more than just breathe life into the drawing – it had also uncovered an indefinite feeling she quickly learned to shut out.

She pours herself a glass of wine and pictures the hue the turquoise lace thong will acquire against the tanned skin of her neighbour's stomach, and a clamour of colour spectrums washes over her brain, which until recently had been grey. She drinks wine until night falls on Barcelona, shrouding the dreams of everyone sleeping. Elena, on the other hand, is fighting the insomnia, uncertainty and anxiety that often visit her and feel like a kind déjà vu that's hard to sift through when it rears its head. She turns off the light in the hope that her nerves will dissolve until they're almost imperceptible, but a faint sound in the apartment next door catches her attention. She gets out of bed and almost instinctively stalks the tiniest traces of sound. They could be footsteps or muffled laughter. Or they could belong to the neighbour she pictures dressed in nothing but her ebony hair. Elena glances at the moon hanging in the sky, as thin as a fingernail in the dark, and the silence broken by the hum of the fridge returns her to a fragile calm.

Elena has been busy drawing since early in the morning. The sound of the doorbell startles her.

'It's Anabel, your new neighbour. The one without the clothesline!'

She opens the door expectantly and is met with the same penetrating, cheerful eyes she remembers from the other day.

'Is now a bad time?'

'Not at all! Come in.'

Anabel cocks her eyebrows and tilts her head in amusement. She looks around the apartment and talks about her new place. As soon as she sees the drawing paper, she starts questioning Elena.

'I'm an illustrator, I work from home.'

'Whoa, they're awesome. I love them!' She says this without stopping still; she touches her hair, slides her hands into her pockets, takes them out, slides them back in, laughs, rambles. The walls of Elena's house thrum as they absorb a life that's foreign to them. 'Have you got salt? I'm a walking cliché, I know. New neighbour comes by to ask for salt...' Elena says nothing, all she can muster is a faint smile. 'I'm a mess. I was supposed to fly to Paris today – I work as a flight attendant – but they've just called to say the airport's closed because of the snow, so I guess I'll be here tonight, and I was about to cook up a quick meal when I thought to myself, shit, I haven't got any salt.'

'Why don't you stay for dinner?' Elena says, under the silent weight of her own audacity.

'I really can't right now, sorry. I'm in a huge rush. I'd be game any other day, though. I love a celebration, and we're new neighbours. Which is a great excuse, don't you think? I'm an easy woman.'

She winks. Elena can't figure out how this gesture fits her tone of voice. Overcome with embarrassment, she dashes into the kitchen, muttering something under her breath. She passes her a cup of salt and Anabel's fingers softly brush her hand. Heart pounding in her throat, Elena looks up into her intoxicating eyes.

'You said your name was Elena?'

'It still is.' They laugh nervously, and salt spills onto the wooden floor of the entrance. The two women kneel, and as one of them apologises and the other says it's nothing, Elena realises without meaning to that Anabel isn't wearing a bra under her grey shirt, where she glimpses a perfect pair of small, round breasts crowned with two, tiny nipples. She forces herself to look away from her shirt and catches Anabel looking at her seriously as she licks a dusting of salt off her finger.

'I'm running late.'

Anabel pulls the door shut from the outside, and when there's no more than a small opening between them, she presses her full lips up to it and whispers 'Thank you for the salt'. Elena stands at the closed door and drinks up the magnificent emptiness of the apartment all in one go.

After a couple of days of being busy with an urgent assignment, embattled with colours, disturbed by memories of her neighbour – to the point of dreaming about her and painting her with brushstrokes of rage and desire – but mostly annoyed at herself for not being able to come to a conclusion, Elena heads up to the rooftop to hang her laundry, and the cold smacks her in the face. She fights against the massive sheet, which the wind stubbornly whips around. Once it's finally taut, she looks up and sees the wavering shadow of a body against the cotton.

'Hi, Elena.' A sliver of fine clothing separates them, and the erratic rhythm of one woman's breathing mingles with the calm cadence of the other's. The incessant beating of Elena's heart pummels her non-stop. It's the starting shot, the chant she thinks she might have finally understood. She takes a step back, ready.

'Sorry, did I scare you?'

Anabel lifts the sheet with a smile. Elena doesn't blink; seized by the inertia that all her reservations had instilled in her over the years, she takes Anabel's face in her hands and kisses her. Anabel's hot, wet lips unclasp in her mouth and she feels two fingers track through her hair. Then, in the middle of this timeless embrace, Elena warily opens her eyes and watches the rooftop meld with lips she imagines are pink. She makes an abstract sketch in her mind and suddenly feels she could paint the rooftops just like this, in every colour.

'It's not snowing anymore. I'm leaving tomorrow,' says Anabel, softly sweeping Elena's hair away from her face and tucking it behind her neck.

She'll make the same gesture a few hours later when, under the warmth of the duvet, their legs entangled, Elena tells her she's always been scared of flying.

Or the worst, but only just

Carlos Zanón

Translated from the Spanish by Annie McDermott

> *We're not the best we could have been.*
> *Or the worst, but only just.*
> Javier Carnicer, 'Humanity'

THERE'S A GUY OUTSIDE a bar who claims you can see whales from Barcelona at dawn. Martí Sales believed it and even put it in a song. Some drunken tall tale, most likely. One of many. Now I'm on a quest to find a taxi. We could drive around Barcelona, head to the beach and see for ourselves if any whales come this way. But maybe it's the delirium tremens talking. Maybe it's those voices hidden in taxi drivers' radios. Or maybe it's just this state of mind called Barcelona.

Cerveza beer.

This universal language, English, Catalan, Spanish and drunk, all rolled into one, and we're bouncing from person to person like the ultimate trick shot, making sure we never pot the black. No more drugs, I just want to walk, to walk for a while down the Ramblas to the sea, and if you spot a taxi, flag it down and it can take us there, to the square and the bar, and the place right outside my old school where Helio was killed.

I'm from here, from this neighbourhood, La Barceloneta. My parents, too.

Fifty euros? No, por favor, Señor Paquistaní, leave us alone.

We're in love and, yes, surely it's possible, please: whales on Barcelona Beach.

Nothing all that serious ever happens in this city: the dumpster fires make headlines then go out by themselves. We just don't want to lose the buzz, the rush, the rich kids thinking they're starting a revolution and the poor kids not realising that this is their city too.

Adéu. Fins demà. I'll call you, okay?

I love this dance, my shoes shuffling on the sawdust in toilets that stink of bleach and beer. Skidding like Helio's feet in his blood, all those years ago. And a song comes on and the singer says he's gay he's a Nazi he's a slag he's a commie he's a fatso he's a fag. Barcelona like a padded cell, soundproofed and consequence-free in that song, in this neighbourhood. Trust me. Demà et truco, I'll call you tomorrow. Yep.

Helio was killed outside the school. A school he never went to. Helio didn't need classrooms or teachers or history or language lessons: he knew everything already and he always had, since before he was even born. The contempt Helio felt for us, the little kids and teenagers hanging around the school gates, was almost physically painful. If you stepped into the street you noticed right away whether or not he was there. His contempt was baseless, limitless. Though not even that was guaranteed. So, you might be walking to school, to the very place he was killed, confident the coast was clear, and then just like that he'd sidle up from the shadows of a doorway nearby, an enormous black spider that felt you catch in its web. Sometimes he looked straight through you. There was no pattern to the humiliation he dealt out. It was cruel, abrasive.

If Helio hadn't died, then even all these years later, now I'm a grown man, a responsible adult, we probably wouldn't be here, and I doubt any whales would show their faces on Barcelona Beach. I was twelve when he was killed. I remember that morning perfectly. Every last detail. And I remember how glad I was that he was dead.

Every weekend, from Thursday to Sunday, Helio was the king of the chiringuitos – the Barceloneta beach bars. One Saturday evening, on the way to one with my parents, I saw him. He was with an older crowd, holding court – he wouldn't have been more than twenty at the time. I stared so hard that he felt me looking and, ever unpredictable, came over, shook my hand, and I think he even exchanged a few words with my father. I felt so proud. But then on Monday when I got to school and saw him at the gates, I waved and he didn't even look at me. The next day, he humiliated me in front of everyone. It was stupid. Cruel and stupid, and I'm not going to go into it now.

Once upon a time, the fishermen were partly paid each day with some of what they'd caught. A tradition developed of grilling the fish right there on the beach. This tradition brought with it wooden shacks, and then beach bars and restaurants and tourists like you, and musicians with accordions, and now I'm coming over all Jarvis Cocker but I hope you won't hold it against me. I'm on a nostalgia kick – nothing to do with Britpop.

This neighbourhood has never been good with authority, but then the authorities have given it nothing but pushes, shoves and cannon fire. It was plotted out with set squares and what you have to remember is that the army and the police go in for Parisian avenues, straight cobbled streets and low-rise buildings, for reasons of visibility. If they're going to shell you from the sea, they don't want too many targets in the way, or too many winding alleys if they're going to shoot you from inland. This was a neighbourhood of fishermen once. Fugitives, too. And labourers. The factories never stopped and there were always people drinking, working, eating, coming and going. That had all disappeared long before I was born but I'm telling you because I think it's nice to know, and for the last time, Señor Paquistaní, we don't want any more goddamn cerveza.

Barceloneta, like New York, was the city that never slept.

My school had a main entrance and a side-way that was kept locked, except on the day Helio was killed. They opened it then so we didn't run into the police, but it just meant we took a couple more minutes to reach the scene of the crime, to see the blood on the pavement for ourselves. He was shot just once. A single bullet in the heart was all it took, like a stake plunged into a vampire. His father was shot as well, but he didn't die. Months later you'd see him out drinking, gripping the bar as if to hold himself upright. He had other children too, but Helio was his favourite. The one who worked with him on building sites. As big a sonofabitch as he swore he had been himself in his younger days.

Leo, Leocadia, would remember Helio. No question. But her bar will be shut by now. You'd have liked it. It's a kind of shrine to this rumba star called Bambino. There are photos of Bambino all over the walls, and in some, he's even with Camarón.[1] Maybe after the whales, we'll swing by. By Bar Leo.

Apparently Helio's father won his wife from her dad in a game of cards. This is according to Damià, a gypsy who was playing as well that night, and who was even called up for a game when Alain Delon was in Barcelona. Helio was ashamed of his mother. In fact, I think what Helio was ashamed of was having a mother full stop. As if he felt more comfortable giving the impression he'd come into the world alone. No one had taught him anything and he'd never been a child, never been innocent, weak, dependent. On the day he was killed, his mother was nowhere to be seen. Or if she was, I don't remember. She'd have been working, most likely. Cleaning houses up in the Zona Alta.

No one was even slightly sorry he'd been killed. Helio was a killer himself, a bully no one ever confronted. Just once, Villanueva's older brother Pruden started on him. He got his arse kicked but he didn't back down, and Villanueva was pretty much left alone for the rest of the year, and the ones after that. I remember Pruden, his face smeared with blood, snot and tears, his shirt ripped to shreds, and Helio gloating with his mates, Alfonso the stupid fat one and Toni the stupid short one, in some doorway not far from the school, lighting a cigarette. I could see his hand shaking. He'd won but he'd taken a few punches and maybe, I think now, the shaking was because if some scrawny loser like Pruden had the nerve to challenge him to a fistfight, it was the beginning of the end. I watched the zippo tremble in his fingers and he saw me looking and stared straight back.

Down there is where Pilar Beltrán used to live. Quiet, nondescript Pilar Beltrán, who decided she was fat one day and never ate again. She ended up a skeleton, nibbling sunflower seeds out of a packet she could barely even lift. Funny to remember her now. All these ghosts that come to populate our lives, and the doorways and street corners of our memories and maybe I'm talking too much, boring you with all this stuff about me, so anyway, where are you from…? That's in the north, right?

The cities of adolescence, of childhood, of youth, are invisible maps full of all those nights when you set out to find yourself and give yourself the slip, wanting to drink, wanting to go wrong again with the right person and, believe it or not, the US Sixth Fleet did a display of the Normandy landings here on this very beach. They took over the slums for a few days, threw out the gypsies, and you had marines landing on the beach, marines flat on their bellies in the sand among the fag butts and seashells. And in fact, it must be true about the whales, because I remember my dad telling me how a particularly large cetacean got lost one day and washed up on one of these beaches. The police had to intervene. The locals came with knives, wanting to slice it up and eat it. This country and this city are animals sometimes. More than you realise.

Helio was killed and his dad was badly wounded, outside the kiosk, not far from Solé's chicken shop. I was friends with Solé's son Albert. He had terrible teeth and an Ibanez bass. We went to see *Rocky II* together. His best friend was this gloomy guy called José Vicente, who called himself a drummer because he could keep time with 'Regatta de Blanc' on his thighs with the palms of his hands. That day he said he heard gunshots and got there before anyone else, when the guy who killed Helio was still holding the gun. Two bodies on the ground, next to the van they usually drove to work. By the time we got to school, everyone had a theory. None of them were true. It wasn't a settling of scores, an unpaid debt or a jealous husband. Or an act of revenge from one of the many people he routinely humiliated every day. It wasn't Pruden. In fact, it was no one. No one important.

Hey, you, yes, now we'll take two cerveza beer. Watch it with the change. Bien. Barcelona, Texas. Adéu. That waiter smoking outside Bar Electricitat looks just like a young Robert De Niro, don't you think?

The fact that no one, not one of us, of all the people who had a reason to kill him, actually killed him, says more than you realise. We never managed to kill Franco, either, or expose our own president's lies. Not one of us took out a gun and aimed it between his eyes and saw his fear, his fear when faced with the justice of the weak, meeting his arrogance head-on. He was killed by some random guy. That's what it said in the papers, so it must have been true.

It was around half seven in the morning and that random guy, someone calm and anonymous, who might have been a policeman or a security guard, had a gun in his glovebox that he'd never used. A load of cars had parked on the kerb overnight and the random guy was boxed in and late. And the vehicle boxing him in was Helio and his father's van. The random guy honking and honking his horn. The clock ticking. The locals grumbling. Helio comes out of the bar where they're having their usual breakfast carajillos and tells the random guy to wait. Five minutes go by, then ten, fifteen, and Helio and his father don't give a crap. They play on the fruit machine. Three lemons. Their lucky day. Then they leave the bar and stroll towards the van, where the random guy's still honking like crazy. Helio's father tells him to get screwed. Helio gives him the finger and stops to scratch his balls. Then he goes over to the car and spits, yellow, on the random guy's windscreen. The random guy clearly has problems. He gets in his car, with Helio still goading him from outside, then he takes the gun from the glovebox, gets back out and points it right at Helio. Helio's father climbs out of the van. Helio says he doesn't have the balls to shoot and the random guy shoots, at the old man as well, puncturing his lung. And then the old man just lies there, motionless, according to José Vicente, the 'Regatta de Blanc' drummer, remember?

This neighbourhood is where the first bullring in Catalonia was built, where the flamenco dancer Carmen Amaya was born and where Helio died outside my school gates and the neighbourhood breathed a sigh of relief, because things were different after that, like in stories when the townspeople kill the dragon. They never say what happens next. What happens next is that no one's afraid of random cruelty or injustice. It's hard to explain. The sand's so fine here, we should take off our shoes. Now all we can do is wait for the whales. Dawn's breaking, kiss me, oh, never mind.

Note

1. José Monje Cruz (1950-1992), better known by his stage name Camarón de la Isla (Shrimp from the Island), was a Spanish Romani flamenco singer, considered one of the all-time greats.

Speed Queen

Jordi Nopca

Translated from Catalan by Mara Faye Lethem

> *'Try now, we can only lose'*
> The Doors, 'Light My Fire'

SHE DOES THE WASHING up while her husband sleeps, dead to the world, on the sofa in front of the blaring telly. It's Monday, so instead of sitting down beside him after tidying the kitchen, to waste the afternoon amid talk shows of dubious quality populated by larger-than-life characters, she fills up her shopping cart with dirty clothes – an ever-so-slight smile etched across her lips – and says goodbye from the doorway to the living room.

'I'm leaving,' she says, with a solemn expression.

And she leaves. She keeps her brow furrowed, feigning annoyance at having to leave the flat at that time of day, until she's in the lift and sees her reflection in the mirror. She can let go of the farce. She smiles again, now openly: she has an hour and a half all to herself, or more precisely, an hour and a half that she should be spending alone, with her gaze fixed on the enormous gunmetal-grey washer as the clothes spin round: her trousers along with her husband's, their shirts, underwear (in his case, stinky underwear), blouses, ratty t-shirts and pyjamas. Sometimes there are also sheets, pillowcases, and tablecloths.

She walks for a couple of minutes until she sees the exoskeleton of the market. On her way to the laundrette, she has to cross Virrei Amat Square, gawk at the dogs being shorn at the groomer's, pass the optician's – where a couple of employees look out with amphibian faces, as if they'd come from another planet – and then the grotty bar where there's always some rough character hanging out in the entrance. Cigarette smoke hangs over that stretch of the street: with a bit of imagination, you could even see how it rises in the shape of skulls, a sign that the benevolent film it inhabits is about to switch genres with the entrance of a gunman.

She is named Maria. Her husband, who remains at home, motionless on the sofa – or perhaps paralysed is a better word choice: he's unable to go out and look for work, and that's been the case for fourteen months now – is named Eduard. They are both 38 years old, and their washing machine is busted. At the laundrette, Carmen greets her with a nod. She always calls her 'honey' with her mouth wide, unabashedly revealing the only five teeth she has left. Her washing machine broke down a few months back too, and that's the least of her problems. It doesn't take a genius to figure out how she earns a living – what sort of bodies and odours she has to deal with every night – and it doesn't take many questions before you notice the alcohol on her breath, mixed with the laundrette's smell of soap and softener. When you walk in, it feels like diving into a fish tank. The walls are blue. Four bubbles painted in one corner heighten the underwater ambience. In the middle of the place, the Speed Queen washers work efficiently or hungrily await their next assignment, drums open.

'Come 'ere, honey, give Carmen a hug,' she demands, arms open.

Two girls in tight jeans and pink shirts struggle to get the soap and softener dispenser to accept their coins, which fall time and again into the small metallic dish where, in theory, their change should come out. Maria hears them cursing in a foreign language and comes over to help. She doesn't have much time – the hour-and-a-half countdown began when she left the house – but she thinks she can solve the problem by swapping a couple of coins with them. They thank her unenthusiastically. From their suitcases filled with dirty clothes hang tags that show clearly where they're from: Cologne, eastern Germany; population one million.

The sound of the washers is slightly narcotic. There is another woman, who fell asleep while trying to solve a word search puzzle, in one of the blue plastic chairs lined up on one side of the laundrette. Maria passes by her to load up a washer drum and add the detergent, which she carries in a half-litre Fanta bottle. They haven't used softener in her house for a while now. When she's done she heads over to the other side of the fish tank to pay. In the laundrette, everything is automatised. The little artificial voice of an employee helps you to successfully complete the transaction. It congratulates you once you have, and if you forget to collect your change it reminds you. The little artificial voice has a Mexican accent.

After the forty-five-minute programme is chosen, the Speed Queen washer awakens from its nap and starts working. Maria leaves the cart alongside a small table where she sometimes sees customers folding sheets. Carmen nods: she'll watch the cart until Maria returns from her mission. The countdown accelerates. It's four thirty. At five fifteen she has to gather the clothes and put them into the dryer.

'See you soon,' she says.

'Of course, honey.'

Instead of going back to Fabra i Puig, she heads up a side street, where all she has to do is dodge smeared defecations and a few gobs of spit that would make a tuberculosis patient proud. The route is not long. She enters the hostel and greets the receptionist, an Ecuadorian man who is always reading the Bible out loud to himself. 'Good afternoon, miss.' She goes straight up to room 21, where he is waiting for her, warming up the bed. She knocks on the door and hears the same two words as always:

'Come in.'

Maria enters and greets him in English before going over and giving him a long, sweet kiss.

'One moment, please,' she says, touching her jacket and pointing to her handbag.

He doesn't release the hug and laughs as he tells her he has no intention of letting her go, because now she's his. She manages to escape him and tosses her jacket and handbag onto the only chair in the room. She takes that moment to lock herself in the bathroom and wash her hands. Maria is a nurse and over the years she's acquired some obsessive habits: one is around smells. The man, with his lush mat of hair combed back and a tattoo on his right arm, could be a typical stinky male. That's not the case. Vladimir keeps himself very clean.

'Why you keep me waiting so long?' he complains when she returns.

He waits naked beneath the sheets. As always, he has made sure to fold his clothes and put them away in the wardrobe that stands by the door, like an enormous copper taking note of this latest crime with the utmost professionalism.

'I am here, finally,' she replies.

'You always have to wait for all the best things.'

Maria starts to take off her clothes, but when she only has her underwear left to remove – flesh-coloured, a bit too functional – she hops into bed: she glimpsed herself in the bathroom mirror and didn't like the colour and texture of her flesh. The mirror in the bedroom continues to spy on the two bodies beneath the sheets. It's been weeks since mere lust has given way to a burning need to touch each other.

Maria is aware that the worst thing that could happen to her would be to fall in love with the Russian pianist. Helena had told her that, more than once, during their night shifts at the hospital.

'Just don't fall in love with that communist, that's the worst thing that can happen to you.'

She would reply, feigning offence: 'Vladi isn't a communist.'

'It's even worse to be a former communist, because that means he's more of a capitalist than you and I put together. I don't even want to imagine him in a mall. He wouldn't be able to control himself.'

'I can't see him going to Heron City.'

'That's probably because Heron City is, like, literally hell. I could see him ravaging El Corte Inglés.'

When she told her the story it was under the condition that she would not say anything to their co-workers. They were in the little room where they keep the bandages and the sedatives, surrounded by packets and the spicy perfume of disinfectants. Helena's mouth hung open for a few seconds.

'Oh my God. Oh my God!' Helena broke with her usual terseness and added: 'You are the worst.'

She had just found out about their first meeting at the laundrette, when Maria had loaded up the Speed Queen and sat down in one of the blue chairs. Normally she would bring a magazine. If Carmen wasn't there, she would read gossip about the glitzy, dirty laundry of the Spanish jetsetters and 'unforgettable' actors and actresses who retired after 'hit careers', or who died, 'consumed' by a 'serious illness.' That afternoon, a stranger had walked in after she'd been reading for a few minutes. He was wearing a worn-out leather jacket and dragging a suitcase with wheels that looked like it had been handed down over three generations of poverty. It was Vladimir, from Saint Petersburg, formerly known as Leningrad – or Petrograd, between 1914 and 1924 – a city of five million inhabitants. She'd noticed him right away. She wouldn't have said anything to him if he hadn't asked for her help: he couldn't quite figure out the instructions on how to pay for a wash. He was struggling to read them in Spanish, but he could barely string a few words together. Maria switched the menu into English and she also changed languages, establishing a strange analogy with the machine. They ended up sitting in the fish tank's blue chairs, submerged in a world of trembling voices and precarious grammar.

'As I listened to him, I realised that, for the first time in a long time, someone was looking at me differently, and I liked that,' she'd said to Helena in the little room filled with bandages and sedatives, opening and closing a box of gauze.

He told her a little bit about Russia. He also said that he earned his living as a pianist and shared a crappy flat in an alley in Horta with three friends. Maybe it was a lie, and Maria was surprised to find herself thinking that, because she shouldn't care whether that man had a wife, a girlfriend, or whatever. He had done who knows how many years of piano at the conservatory, but for the time being he was playing every night at a bar in the Gothic Quarter, with a saxophonist, a double bassist, and a drummer. She was married, since she was twenty. She had shared almost half her life with the same man, Eduard, who was unwilling to lift a finger to find work and only had eight months left of unemployment benefits. She should have explained all that, but in her rudimentary English, it would have sounded even worse than it was. Her head was spinning when he stepped outside to have a smoke. She saw how he was looking her over from the doorway of the laundrette: a shark studying the best way to gobble down its prey, not even considering that the prey might offer itself up, with no resistance, because it felt like it, or because, simply, it was a fish filled with poison. The first day they only kissed, with the sounds of the spin cycle whirring in the background.

They agreed to meet up again the following Monday, at the same time. He looked down at his shoes, intimidated. Maria noticed and took it as a very good sign.

She spent a week imagining how she would tell him that she's married and that, as such, they had to be very discreet. When the time came, she left the house with her grocery cart filled with clothes after saying goodbye to Eduard, and she almost changed her mind. It would have been a mostly symbolic act: confining herself to her home – hiding her head in her shell – when really she was vibrating with anticipation at the thought of seeing the pianist with his leather jacket again. That day he showed up with his hair as neatly combed as when they'd met, but in a turtleneck sweater that fit better with the stereotype that Maria might have about Russia and its inhabitants. They shook hands in greeting. They were lucky in that there was only one young woman in the laundrette, and she was gathering up her clothes from the dryer, too focused on her folding to pay attention to the brief speech Maria gave Vladimir. She told him more or less everything she'd planned to: that she was 'happily' married and that she loved her husband very much, that what had happened the other day had been 'an accident' and that 'obviously' she was not 'easy.'

'I understand,' he answered.

He paused for a moment and inhaled before asking her if she wouldn't rather talk about all that somewhere quieter. He indicated the bar across the street by shifting his head horizontally in that direction.

'Maybe we can go to a more quiet place.'

She went over to the machine to pay the four euros for her wash. Her hands were shaking as she put the coins in, clink-clink. She heard Vladimir approaching from behind. His footsteps suddenly stopped. 'Please,' he said.

That entreaty was expeditious: he probably would not

repeat it. Maria thought her answer over for a few seconds as the machine spat out a receipt, the last step before the washer was set into motion. When she turned round, she found that he was too close to her, and her expression forced him to take a few steps back. She waited a bit longer before resolving the question that had left Vladimir with his mouth open, observing her with pleading eyes. After pressing the start button, she divulged her answer. 'OK. Let's go.'

The bar across the street was a dark den, populated by construction workers, painters, plumbers and electricians nourishing their bodies with beers and liquor. When they entered, Maria still saw the blue of the laundrette on their faces, but also on the walls and the motorcycling trophies locked in a case. She began to think that now the world was tinged that colour, not because she saw it that way, but because it had changed hue. In that parallel reality, she ran no risk of running into someone she knew from the neighbourhood.

The barman made two white coffees. As they drank them, they decided to meet up the following week in a nearby hotel to get to know each other 'a little more'. Their meetings could never last longer than the forty-five minutes the wash cycle took. She made him promise that, and he accepted with a severe nod. Deal. The voices that spoke during that entire transaction weren't Maria's or Vladimir's, but belonged instead to a strange presence that emerged from inside the woman and the man, from both of their bodies at the same time, while in the background a cumbia played, and in it a voice that was both festive and indignant sang: *Why'd you change your name? Why are you telling me that now?* They searched for a place to meet on his mobile phone, a Samsung with a slow reaction time – leaden – just like the conversations going on around them. There weren't many places nearby. The second address they looked at won them over because of its proximity to the laundrette. They went onto its website and she read out loud the only comment, in a grey-coloured rectangle:

'We had a wonderful stay, the rooms are very clean and very comfortable. A quick hop from the centre of Barcelona.'

Even though it was 'only' a hostel, it was the perfect place. A double was reasonably priced and didn't vary much between the high and low seasons. That meant that it wasn't as quick of a hop from the city centre as that customer in the rectangle – someone named Bea, twenty-one years old and from Seville – had promised. But Maria and Vladimir had no interest in visiting the Sagrada Família or the Pedrera, or the Picasso Museum, or taking a stroll in the Raval. They just wanted a little privacy to let things run their course.

'I've never been with an artist,' Helena told her, during the confession in the little room filled with bandages and sedatives. 'It must be special.'

If Maria had had a way with metaphors, she could have said that the man played her just like a grand piano: he began with an almost indifferent slowness, but as the concert really got underway, he could even be violent, pounding on the keys with a fury drawn from some unfathomably deep part of him. Maria decided to keep it clean and just nodded her head.

'It's special. It's different.'

She had no way of knowing this, but the only grand pianos Vladimir had played were the ones in the Saint Petersburg Conservatory. Since passing his final exam he'd had to make do with Casio and Yamaha keyboards. In the bar in the Gothic Quarter where he played every night, they didn't appreciate him and he earned a pittance, which he then had to share with the other three musicians.

After a quick shower, Maria takes the Fanta bottle filled with detergent from her bag, pours a little on her hands and washes them, making as much foam as she can. That way, the only scent Eduard will notice when she gets home will be automatically associated with the laundrette. It's ten minutes after five and time to go pick up the clothes.

'Bye-bye,' she says, bringing her index and middle fingers to her forehead, and sweeping them horizontally forward. Vladimir takes her hand. He places a sticky kiss on the back of it.

'I'll miss you.'

His words are redundant: his eyes overflow with yearning, as does the hair on his chest, and the tattoo on his right arm which, instead of being a mermaid stretched out on a rock, transforms into Maria in a bikini, about to dive into the water during their first vacation together (they talked about it once, in an embrace, while he ran his fingers through her hair).

She has to leave. They kiss one last time beside the wardrobe near the door to the room. He repeats that he will miss her.

'Me too,' she admits.

She walks down the hostel's stairs and says goodbye to the receptionist, who continues reading the Bible, or pretending to. One day she should ask him which are his favourite passages, but she's afraid to make too strong of an impression on him, and later run into him in some neighbourhood shop, or the market, when she's with Eduard, and have the receptionist adopt the rage of an Old Testament prophet to proclaim, publicly, that she is an adulteress. He would surely not mince his words.

Mrs Carmen is no longer at the laundrette. The two young women in tight jeans and pink t-shirts she helped earlier wave and giggle. If they were in Cologne they'd probably greet her with less mirth. She waves back and heads directly to the clothes in the washer. After being with the pianist she moves more slowly: every week she gets home a little later, each week she cares a little less. When the thirty-minute dryer cycle starts it's already 4:38. She sits down in one of the blue chairs and pulls out her magazine. She pages through it as she reconstructs her time spent with Vladi. The caresses. The thrusts. Sometimes she comes round again and realises she's gnawing on her lower lip.

'Just don't fall in love with that communist, that's the worst thing that can happen to you.'

She remembers Helena's words before mentally returning to the small room he must have already left. He has never let her pay for the hostel. He says that he can cover it with the tips he gets at the bar, but he doesn't say that he struggles to survive on what he makes, and that there are days when he skips lunch or dinner so that he can afford the luxury of their Mondays.

'Vladi isn't a communist.'

The day they met, Maria had to take a look at an online encyclopaedia to find out a few things about Russia.

'It's even worse to be a former communist, because that means he's more of a capitalist than you and I put together. I don't even want to imagine him in a mall. He wouldn't be able to control himself.'

She'd tried searching online for images of Vladimir Putin in a mall, but the only thing she'd found were t-shirts, keychains, flags and even knife sheaths with the president's face, often wearing military attire and sunglasses. A head of state in sunglasses brought to mind those dogs in awkward costumes that starred in a soft drink advert.

Another woman just walked into the laundrette. She's wearing a black suit jacket and carries a large plastic bag with the clothes she's come to wash. It must be her first time there. If she had even a tiny bit of experience she'd know that, in a bag like that, her clothes would end up a wrinkled mess. Maria observes her, keeping the magazine open on her lap. At first, the woman doesn't know how to pay and she curses, but she must be proud, because she never asks for help. She reads the written instructions on one wall and figures it out. She jams her clothes into one of the wash drums and presses the button to set the Speed Queen into motion. She sits down two chairs away from Maria. Now, finally, she says 'Good afternoon.'

'Good afternoon.'

She grabs her mobile and types something into it. Almost immediately she brings it to her ear and calls someone. Maria, who pretends to be reading an article about Queen Letícia's beauty secrets, can't help but prick up her ears and listen to what the stranger is saying.

'Cristina? Hey, hi, is this a good time? You sure? OK. We'll just talk until the physiotherapist calls you in... You are not going to believe what happened to me at the office. Yeah, yeah, today, this morning, just after I got in. Well, actually, it didn't happen to me, but the cleaning lady told me about it. It's insane, it's wild.'

The woman's hysterical tone is hard to bear, but it's the only way Maria can hear what happened to her at the office. It begins with her saying good morning to the cleaning lady and, when she sees her face, asking her if she's feeling well, to which she responds that she's fine. But the office worker insists because she's polite, especially with those on a lesser rung in the work hierarchy. Lowering her voice, the cleaning woman says that her problem has to do with one of the women's lavatories. The smell that comes out of it, even with the door closed, because she hasn't dared to open it and isn't going to, is horrible. The office worker wrinkles her nose. She explains that she'd seen 'real horrors' in the office lavatories and that it can only be because there are 'a lot of nasty people' working there, and in the privacy of the loo they don't hold back. 'I'd like to see if they'd do that in their own house,' she continues. The cleaning lady observes her with wide eyes. Perhaps she doesn't quite understand what she's saying, or she doesn't comment because she doesn't want to speak badly about anyone: she's only hired to come in from 7 to 9am three days a week. She sees nothing, she hears nothing, she is a spirit that holds no grudges. The office worker has to insist to get her to confess, in a hushed voice and with a slight Romanian accent, why she refuses to enter the toilet: the stench she smelled is a human foetus.

Maria nearly leaps out of her chair. A human foetus in a toilet? She fixes her eyes on the magazine. Queen Letícia's beauty secrets are the perfect shield to allow her to continue eavesdropping on that story without drawing attention to herself.

'So crazy, right?! Then she goes, "It's not the first time I've come across one." I'm sure she's seen all sorts of things in her country. Yeah, yeah, I already told you, she's Romanian.'

The office worker continues the story. Her curiosity piqued by the possibility that the cleaning lady was right, she gets up and heads over to the door to the lavatories. When she is in front of the sink, her hand on the golden knob that will allow her into the toilet, she feels unable to turn it, because the stink is simply unbearable. She turns round and goes back out into the corridor, where the cleaning lady is waiting for her – for the first time she notices her turquoise uniform. 'You agree something's going on in there?' She nods. It's worse than she was imagining. They can't go in there, they have to go get someone else. But who? The cleaning lady repeats that 'there's a foetus in there, a human life' and that it's 'a very serious subject'. At the same time, she clearly states that she doesn't want 'problems'.

The office is practically empty. They only find one computer tech on the far side, looking at his screen with headphones on and a concentrated expression, his bald pate gleaming and a pen hanging from his lips. He is watching a Britney Spears video: 'Womanizer'. Perhaps because he was caught red-handed, he listens to the small speech that his co-worker elaborates based on what she'd been told by the cleaning lady, who corroborates throughout with supportive interjections: 'ah', 'aha', 'agh', 'aho'. 'No problem,' he says when she's finished. 'Let's go have a look'. The computer tech leads the expedition to the women's lavatories. The two women wait outside while the man enters the off-limits toilet and lifts the lid. He doesn't say anything for a few seconds. 'Do you want to come in?' he asks. Both of the women, at the same time, ask him what he found. 'Half-rotted fish scraps. Someone must have got rid of their old lunch leftovers'. He flushes before either the office worker or the cleaning lady dare confirm what he said. 'Yuck, what a stink,' he admits when he comes out of the toilet. 'Some people have no shame.'

Maria's dryer cycle ends as the woman finishes the story. She continues on the phone, now on a strictly work-related topic, as Maria gets up from the chair to gather her clothes. When she's finished, she walks past the woman and says goodbye, contrite. She gets no response. That night, after eating a plate of vegetables and hake, she will have to run to the toilet to vomit, and when she looks in the mirror after brushing her teeth, as she sips a bit of water, she will wish with all her might to have a problem inside her, one that would grow for months until she could give birth to it at the hospital. But she still isn't sure who she wants to be the father.

Other People's Partners

Gonzalo Torné

Translated from the Spanish by Ruth Clarke

I NEVER EXPECTED MY return from London to cause a sensation. Sure, all those years had gone by, but I'd stayed in touch by email, we saw each other at Christmas, I knew what my nearest and dearest were doing with their lives. But it didn't cause so much as a splash. I'm not saying they didn't listen to me, they paid me hours of polite attention, but I guess it didn't exactly feel great to find out that all my years in London could be condensed into a few stories that only took half an afternoon to tell. If ever I thought it would be easy to keep my London habits and views – that they had become deeply enough ingrained – now that I couldn't go to Terry or Iris for a refresher, or hang out in Green Park, or walk along the South Bank, it became apparent that they were tied to very specific spaces, and that without those spaces they would languish like creatures whose habitat is unexpectedly changed by deforestation or a diverted river.

Two weeks in Barcelona was all it took to shift the balance between the two cities in my life. I couldn't stroll around like a tourist, fresh new streets didn't open out before my eyes; as soon as I looked at those pavements, a series of experiences would jump up to meet my senses (expectations, disappointed words, passions) only to go straight back to their usual place in my emotional framework. My London experiences were still there, but they couldn't compete in intensity; the time that contained them carried less weight, I had invested it in an exotic currency that was devaluing before my eyes.

It can't have helped that I came back from London with no job, and that the only idea I had about my future was a handsome husband who could only be taken seriously if you looked at him from a distance. It really doesn't matter how much you drank, how much you danced, the kisses, the conversations, the tiny social victories, all that drama you indulged in, day in day out for months, when you try to calculate your own worth, when you feel the urge to dust off your recent achievements. It's a bit absurd, but there it is.

Of course, Barcelona didn't feel like home either. It's not that the city had changed, the layout was still the same, wedged between two impassable rivers; Diagonal still cut through the blissful latticework of the Eixample district; the major monuments were just where I'd left them, radiating their fame; Aragón and Gran Vía still ran parallel to each other with their feel of ancient streets, and special buses could take you to the Carmel hills and to the far reaches of the port, with its abandoned railway lines, containers and seabirds. I think the feeling of displacement, of slight dizziness, that accompanied me through the months of readjustment, came from the closed restaurants and bookshops, the new fabric on the shop awnings, the cafes nobody went to anymore, the new look and asphalt of the plazas, the changing rhythm of people you find where you once wouldn't, changes in population, in the cultural composition of places. The drawing of the city was the same, but now it seemed smudged, as if a distracted child had rubbed their hand over the ink.

In any case, I didn't feel the dizzying euphoria of homecoming. I started working really hard to reintegrate into the only scrap of earth where I could possibly belong; I'm not strong enough to live without roots, even if they are too soft to really force themselves into the ground. I was too busy trying to get out of my own private labyrinth to deal with the social concerns of Amanda's new friends, so I let Álvaro entertain me, that's one of the things that worked out best for me. It amuses me the way my little brother, the novelist, manages to look at you as if you're transporting a substance that will determine the survival of the entire human race. He can keep his face perfectly still, although a twitching foot gives away his impatience and I know it won't be long before I see him hopping from group to group, in animated conversation, protected by that imperceptible, dismissive veneer. I can endorse any unpleasant thing anyone says about Álvaro without losing an ounce of my regard for him, and it doesn't surprise me, it's always been like that.

'Working?'

'You could call it that.'

'Don't you get just a little bit bored?'

'Well, that's because people have got used to not saying anything in public that would upset their mothers and spouses. They get corrupted, the day they feel the urge to say something juicy it gets distorted as soon as it hits the inevitable wall of psychobabble. But if you could see them on the inside.'

'You're kidding me.'

'Look at them: dating couples, friends, married couples, those words are like round walls that protect a tiny world of unsuspecting emotions from prying eyes. Every one of those duos is putting on a show for the angels. A device to pierce through those defences and take a look inside, that would be priceless, you could flog it at Christmas.'

'What unspeakable things are you doing with Laia?'

'You're an idiot, Clara. You've always been the biggest idiot of the three, that's why we love you so much. When are you going to introduce me to your husband?'

'Boyfriend.'

'When?'

'Soon. Do you never go up and ask them?'

'About their innermost secrets? Why would I do that? I can come up with them in my imagination, it's more hygienic.'

'Speaking of mothers, are you still not calling her?'

'That role does not suit you, you're too subtle, you'll never compete with Amanda there, that's the only place she'll always win.'

In practice, what happened is that he would leave me alone at parties, in rooms, in new bars, steamrollered into conversations held together by a shared knowledge of trees and cereals that I was unaware of: interests had shifted, and I was not up to speed on the new network of relationships. The overwhelming feeling was one of arriving in the middle of a party, when everyone has already been drinking for hours. Of course, alcohol helps, and a G&T administered at just the right moment can shed light on a conversation and soak up your reservations, but all that lay beneath those glimmers was an accumulation of idle afternoons, which gradually reduced down to nothing and left me with a whimsical collection of loose ends.

I think I was disappointed to realise that my long-lost friends had appropriate goals for the times: paying bills, organising the shopping, supporting parents who were starting to fade, pushing through the days, carving out leisure time, saving energy, the sophistications and civilised tedium of the weekend. Our conversations got bogged down in an exchange of balances: finances, affections, labour. They talked about holidays, mobile phones, cars, the price of oranges. They had settled into a cell in this tiny social network, they were adapting well to life at lukewarm temperatures. I didn't dare tell them that their switched-off tone, how happily they let their imaginations spin in ever-narrowing circles, depressed me. Equally, I would have had no comeback if they'd asked me what I was doing better than them. As if I wasn't worried about the rent, one step away from asking for help, wishing for a new husband so we could start something together, anything. We lived in a privileged space, protected by a social and legislative system, surrounded by incredible mechanical gadgets; there we were, somehow it worked. I suppose I should be grateful that the image I projected from under that gauze of constant worry was a model of politeness.

Later, they started to open up.

Irina and I had tried dating for a while, but it didn't end well. I met her when I was trying to figure out whether I liked boys or girls better, and I felt like it was my fault that it didn't work out. I was rushing down Roger de Llúria when I ran into her, her red hair sitting like a crown on top of her slim, nervous figure. She called out a pet name I'd forgotten, kissed my cheek, and struck up a conversation, standing in the middle of the street under an ominous sky. As I listened to her, I struggled to place exactly when we'd stopped replying to each other's emails. I related it to an impulse in the authoritarian part of my spirit to be more serious, to stop sharing all my indiscretions, but I liked this girl, and I'm not sure I stopped liking her.

I hadn't realised, and here she was, telling me about her film career. In the early days, we used to watch a lot of films together. The cinema has always been my favourite plan: the silky darkness tempering my nerves, the fiction glowing on the fabric window; I love how the golden award wreaths look like circles of wheat. Irina would occasionally convince herself that her vocation was to be a director, taking notes on the films we watched, arranging her ideas into files, scripting scenes without a hint of talent; in writing, her tenderness would quickly drive her towards sentimentality and cloying emotions, a good soul.

Of course, this never mattered to me; what I liked about her were things like the way she put on her socks, pretended to have a stomach ache so I would take care of her and bake apples for her, the way she asked me to scratch her, the spirit with which she would devour a litre of ice cream sitting on the floor and then ask me to kiss her. What I liked about her was her sensitivity that got bolder, as if the solution to life's problems could only come from her own pipe dreams, this spirit that would burst into tears of joy, sadness, excitement, all because life exists, life that begins and continues for a time, and they'd saved one, a whole one, just for her. She would take me by the arm, drag me out of the house, force me to go with her to places where she managed to find a hundred different ways to declare her undying love. Irina was unstoppable at parties, her secret weapon was that tiny diesel tank she'd fitted in her back, it never let her down. Backchat drove her crazy, and she knew how to sabotage my pensive moods. She would tickle me, grab my jumper, bite me in the street.

She told me that she had hovered like an electron around the cinematic mass until she found a free orbit in its complex gravitational field. She had specialised in 'photography', she went where she sensed she could sneak in, the men liked having her around, she knew how to handle other girls, she dropped a few well-known names I didn't recognise, nobody gets paid, she was still excited by appearances. She looks to be doing alright. She's got good genes and on top of that she enjoys sweating in the gym and 'raw food' diets. It seemed only right that I should make a joke about the thickness of her orange acetate glasses, it was an attempt to stop the casual meeting from affecting me too much, it didn't work, I tried to say goodbye, but she was heading in the same direction as me, and as we were walking up to the little square where Diagonal crosses Bailén, it started to rain. We didn't have umbrellas and I thought we'd make a run for the tube station at Verdaguer, but she grabbed my arm with the same force she used to keep me in her parents' bed for an extra half hour, to prolong that atmosphere of pleasant complicity that went far beyond the effect of any of the words used to describe the love between women.

We ducked into Bauma with our spring jackets dripping wet, that laugh was new, we ordered a couple of drinks, she left her glasses folded on the table, tried to reach me with her naked, greenish gaze, she was flirting with me. I didn't want to hurt her, it just didn't do anything for me. Her face crumpled to show the remains of a grudge. I think she was about to put it into words, but she raised her hand to her lips to stifle a giggle, and that gesture did yank me out of place. It sent me back to the day when I saw Irina walk into the classroom, following in the footsteps of a hairy boyfriend, with a chair above her head; a very thin girl, with eyes shrunken by myopia, who would stare incredulously at her hands as we smoked in the afternoon sunshine, carefree and glowing, surprised and grateful that these waves of warm feelings were for her.

When we finished school, her shyness turned upside down and she suddenly felt obliged to shock me, nothing entertained her more than talking about sex, the extent of her appetite for filthy details was worthy of a Flemish master; you know how I get along with Álvaro, I feel comfortable in the role of the sensible older sister. It was a surprise that during this first act of our reunion she didn't show her dirty side at all. It turned out that she didn't have anything too exciting to report. She had given up playing games with women.

'I chose motherhood. I joined the big leagues, with the men.'

She knocked back her G&T, made that sound of quenching thirst that I don't think there is a word for, shook the remains of the ice. It was only 7pm, and the last of the daylight was moving across the sky; on the pavement men slowed their pace to stare at us, one day it will be unthinkable to start drinking at this hour, that will be sad.

'We loved standing out. I didn't have your mind or your eyes or your fear of looking ridiculous. I learned how to get them to warm to me, even though I was more sharp-tongued than approachable, I didn't have to go through the basic exercises, I made myself stand out because I was precocious, being restless helped me get through adolescence. Nowadays it would be difficult to stand out for being the one with no inhibitions who talks about cocks all the time. Girls these days, I see them on set, they have phantom minion jobs in catering or make-up, they know the names of porn actresses, studied Humanities, went to private film schools with a ton of acronyms. I made friends with this little Slavic girl, she would open the papers so at least we'd have something to talk about, very careful and well-trained, one of those girls who, in our day (let me say that again "our day", it makes me so happy), would not have had to tone down her exuberance.

'I didn't bring boyfriends into the conversation, since I thought she was keen and on the hunt; spend five years away from your post-teen tribe, and you start to forget how to read the signs. She did have a guy, one of those Latinos with a glint in their eye like an aggressive teardrop sliding down a dull background. His arms hung limp, a portent of flabbiness, he was funny, and if he encouraged the girl to dress up like a trophy, or bow her head, it wasn't out of malice, his optic nerves had to connect sensations to a brain that could only codify reality into a volley of stiff, forceful words: "Look at me", "mine", "yours", "I want it", "swap", "be careful".

'I can understand why a girl would fantasise about sleeping with any kind of life form, even I'm tempted to one day savour the pleasure of using my boobs to dominate a creature like that, but of course the intimacy implied between the Slavic girl and the brute went down the old submission route. The girl didn't strike me as dumb, it's just that macho men are back, if they ever went away, it's exactly what you'd expect her to do if she doesn't want to end up isolated from social contact. Every time she takes off those sunglasses that cover half her face, I'm silently rooting for her, hoping that I won't see the marks, that she's gone another day without testing his temper. She's going to have to be careful if she's managed to convince herself that she really does love him.

'When you think about it, we grew up in a very different climate. We went into those classrooms full of Brothers, Fathers, Marists and Salesians and Marianists like an alien invasion, a feminine perfume with the power to revive evolutionary lines in steep decline; sensitive guys who spent their adolescence openly harassed or locked in the toilets of their all-boys schools, guys who were ripe targets for humiliation, until they could move into civilian housing, they joined forces with us. We loved their dreamy expressions, the speed of their complex minds, what they could do to you with their words. Intelligent was the new sexy. Don't laugh, Clara, I'm not making this stuff up, I've given it some real thought.

'The innocent version is that boys could play with dolls and we could play wargames. The twisted version was that we couldn't let our male friends or partners treat us like delicate creatures anymore, we had to roll up our sleeves, abandon our homely cloister (suppress intense organisational and decorative urges that had made their way down the generational rivers in the gene boat), and compete in the masculine territory known as the labour market. And them? Well, it was enough for them to stage a couple of steps towards ultimate equality. Our effort came at a price, theirs was instantly applauded. They showed some charity, while we were compelled to get to work in places as diverse as the dining room, the office, between the sheets, on the street (first rule of female thermodynamics: if you neglect your physical self, social death is inevitable), and motherhood. Sweet, strong, understanding, productive, all at, more or less, the same time. They were told that in exchange for a quick surface clean of the bathroom, the weight of household income would no longer fall on their shoulders;

we had a riddle thrown in our faces that had no answer, that went to the very core of existential organisation. I admit that there are thousands of mean, silly, lazy girls, but guys aren't much better! And we're the ones who get invited to this saga of frayed nerves, to the golden decade of anti-anxiety drugs.

'Sandro was a specialist in sexual matters, and I suppose I was the most amenable girl on hand. Don't think we left it all to intuition, it was thoroughly documented, pop style, across a range of reference levels: Freud, Bataille, that ubiquitous turd de Sade, *Your Erogenous Zones*, *Karma Sutra* (illustrated), *Primera Línea, Cosmopolitan, 69 for Everyone*. Our conversations were playful. And Sandro wasn't satisfied with just enjoying his experiences on top of and underneath me, not at all, our intercourse was the *exemplum* of ecumenical influence. The forefront of a national transformation. Sandro suggested putting an end to centuries of unsatisfied women, freeing us from tedious, parochial copulation, redeeming us from the depredations of the castrating myth of the vaginal orgasm. You already know the mindset that seeks to convert an individual habit into collective enterprise, well now it has gone further. You have dog lovers, fans of driving on two wheels, recycling enthusiasts with their six different brightly coloured bags. With a bit of effort, they always manage to set their various obsessions into the same fanatical paste. There's also the fact that we need a cause close to our heart, there's that too. Of course, because it was about sex, Sandro got behind it and made it kind of funny. I don't know what things are like in London, but in this city, you don't have to leave the house to flaunt your cosmopolitanism, it's positively encouraged, wrapped up in the land registry; for lack of any more tumescent concerns, in Barcelona there's no idiot who isn't replicated twice over in our sex dramas, of course Sandro was from Ciudad Real, and that must be a very strange place.

'The truth is we were very well equipped: gels, lubricants, belts, straps, specialist (and indeed, highly specialist) videos… stopping to buy fresh vegetables lost its halo of everyday innocence. In short: Sandro was an orgasm geek. I simply got tired of coming eight times a night in the name of true gender equality. And he took offence. He accused me of not being able to get over my gender-based repression on a more than superficial level, and I said goodbye. A year or two later, I got sick of taking care of myself and thinking of myself as a singular creature, and I married the most sensible guy I could find. You could have helped me, Clara, but you were busy with other people. Part of me is still upset with you, furious, we could have carried on writing at least. Even when I was your favourite, I was appalled to hear you say that no one can live without letting go of dead weight, why make things so clear, I don't know. Don't get me wrong, I don't hold it against you, you have no idea how happy I am to see you; that's the bad thing about attractive people, without being their partner or their lover, it's impossible to keep hold of them the way you'd like.'

The new guy was some kind of engineer and had done lighting work for two or three short films they shot in Born.

'Multicultural. Batukas, hippies, those Brazilian dances where they look like they're doing stretches and hanging in the air, playing the bongos. Lights are his hobby. He worked in a bank, the major accounts department. You must know what that's like.'

I went on his Tumblr, a gallery of technical exercises, school compositions, socially charged stereotypical nods (homeless people, street vendors, low houses on wide avenues), melancholy perspectives (rain, twilight) on well-known cities. Internet users go on and comment and leave links to broadcast their 'work', cite some 'big name', and most of them are too excited by the exchange of routine compliments to learn the job, to calculate the likelihood of one of their ideas being successful.

'You know. Neutral, clean, strong, formal.'

She met him in a queue for the cinema (a rom-com) and they slept together (in his small, bright, neat loft apartment) and Irina told him about her future plans (improvised) and her immediate plans: what she was going to do to him right there, as soon as they got out of bed.

'I thought I was going to kill him, but I hadn't bargained on the energy boost from his red-blooded transformation.'

This guy's vigour had taken her by surprise. She was excited by his proportions, how clumsily he pounced on her hips, and flipped her over to her ass, looking like he was about to devour her, the boy scout spirit with which he approached every anatomical possibility Irina offered him.

Moving in together cut them off at the peak of their erotic bonanza.

'Roberto was horrified by the idea and gave me the usual list of misgivings. He hadn't learned anything about what girls weren't expected to do anymore: cooking, shopping, laundry, ironing and detergent were alien to him, his mum took care of all that. And I get it, how was this big kid, who was perfectly polite, and who dedicated the best part of his day to adjusting decimal places in Mephistophelean accounts, meant to have any idea that his girlfriend was going to renounce all those ambitions, that I was going to turn my back on the rights won by my gender, that I was crazy for locking myself away with that body tempered by intellectual conformity, locking myself away with him?

'I'm not going to justify myself. I've spent a decade and a half dragging my sorry little body around parties and receptions and brunches attended by guys who never warn you when they're about to make fools of themselves, and girls desperate to show off their ideas, which they just gathered at the other side of the room; going all out to maintain the intensity and tension, rattling around to keep up with the incessant flow of looks, ideas and words... People take drugs, drink, get tattoos, do all kinds of things with our hair, go from party to party.... and we're getting closer and closer to becoming ordinary drunks, in the realms of the underdose, the kind of loser that wouldn't know what the end of a party looks like, real dweebs. So, when the deciding moment in my life came, the only rabbit with countercultural fur that I could pull out of my hat, the only subversive action I could think of, was to go and live with a decent man and take care of him, just like mum. And you know what? I'm not bad at it.'

Three happy years together, supporting each other, Irina had managed to finish a script. *A script*. Ludicrous plans make her ecstatic.

When they talk about having kids, Irina still feels there's something fantastical about the idea; their lives have a certain amount of slack, their work days are far from exhausting. Among the pleasures anticipated from motherhood, she realises they're going to need more money, to move house, to cut down the number of hours she has to herself; a clear prediction of the sacrifices, she feels bad for not being able to find emotional balance, she doesn't believe him when he says, as he walks like a beast in underpants towards the fridge, that they will split the load.

'Sandro wanted to re-educate women, one by one, but with the whole gender in mind, starting with the strict and arbitrary discrimination of what is good and what is bad; if we didn't work out (according to him), it was because my emotional framework was too fragile to handle the impact of reality. What nonsense! I'm not afraid of being free, if I'm a victim of anything, it's the discord between much-lauded social freedom and technological progress. Didn't you see it on television? In 150 years, they will be able to develop a human foetus outside the womb. You put the egg in a bell jar, and nine months later, they bring it to us, clean, healthy and vaccinated. I'm just asking for another twenty years, and they won't give it to me.'

I told her about the clinics where they do natural births and Joan-Marc's suggestion that I should give birth in my own bed, with towels that he had steamed himself, supervised by a midwife. They think that a baby coming into the world soaked in the juices of childbirth is less traumatic than a clean room smelling of anaesthetic; their little walnut of a brain emulsifies as they form impressions and develop a sense of familiarity if the air in their first breath contains the sweat, skin, hair and cells of their parents.

'Four years without incident, without a slip. I'd made a life with a machine who had German efficiency and an erection attachment. I specialised in wrapping his reliable strength in silky fantasies. And he wasn't one of those that go around punching the walls when you fob them off because you simply have something else on your mind. He was dull sometimes, but level-headed. We still like sitting in the dark in summer with the windows open watching films. He smells good when he sweats.'

She let go of her glass and smiled at me. If it was a hint, I didn't get it.

'He still has his hobbies from his single days. Once a month he goes out for dinner with the rest of his university crew, I assume they talk about RAM and ROM memory, software and chips and silicates – and about girls, in the inimitable style of married men. I try not to imagine the details of their conversations. Anyway, I can't get to sleep those nights, I can't relax until I hear the whine of the elevator, his keys, the way he thinks he's opening the door gently, while I weigh up the benefits of sulking and end up opting for a smile; Roberto takes off his shoes, kisses me, and lets me talk him into having a shower before he gets into bed, even though it's two or three in the morning, but I just love the idea that he's going to get naked and soaped up for me, that I get to sleep snuggled up against his clean skin.

'That's how I knew something was wrong when he skipped the routine and switched on the bedroom light. Specks floated in front of my eyes, I rubbed them and found him sitting on the edge of the bed, giving me a glassy stare. I covered my chest with the sheet, after nearly four years of living together, shame sprang up quickly and ran through the muscles in my neck. He hardly drinks, and alcohol has a sedative effect on his body, it's like mud that slows down his motor skills and slackens his smile.'

She thought his digestion was acting up again.

'I knew Roberto had a photo of me on his mobile, maybe two. What I didn't know was that whenever he got the chance, he'd launch into a monologue about his partner's attributes, and that this was an illustrated talk. The following day, I inspected the pictures and they were only slightly indecent. Irina reaching for a jar of cocoa powder, Irina panting after a workout, Irina walking around in her bra with a piece of toast in her hand. Everyday poses, practical, parts of domestic life. The tilt of the camera, the angle, the effect, the precise second he chose to shoot were studied to highlight the curves and points of, what do they call it, ah yes, the female form. That's right, perversion is in the eye of the beholder!

'Before I remembered that the correct reaction was to rebuke him for being childish, for being cheesy, for flashing my ass around without letting me join in the game, I felt kind of proud. It didn't even cross my mind that the subject of the reproach was me, that I was the one who was being asked to explain themselves.

'His stupid boys' nights, the meetings of their 'cultural association' dedicated to flaunting mummified shreds of their youth, always have guest stars, passing colleagues. And one of these nouvinguts[1] decided to respond to the two hours that the Major Accounts Department's very own Lewis Carroll had spent showing off his better half (since that was me, I hope Roberto put some effort in) with the unexpected announcement that he knew me. He gave him a grand tour of ancient legends, at the pale heart of which was me, from a time when that kind of news fell like manna from heaven on hordes of adolescent boys to fuel their masturbatory fury.'

Roberto asked for proof and the guy gave it to him.

'That man (short, fat, with frontotemporal androgenetic alopecia: beyond hope) had an anecdote up his sleeve where he starred as my partner. We were floating in a public swimming pool, under a caramel afternoon sun, when the adolescent Irina took an inflatable from a bather with the smooth outline of that stomach now deformed by fat and, without looking him in the eye, she is supposed to have touched the area previously numbed by the obscenities he was whispering in her ear. I was on the verge of jumping out of bed to yell at him, ask him what the hell kind of stupid story this was, what corner of the poor lunatic's imagination had come up with that, how could Roberto believe him?

'"Cruel notes, Turkish daggers beneath the pillow, curtains in the breeze, and a sickle moon!" an impressive summary of the disadvantages of marrying a mind chequered by years of regurgitating equations. What would be next? A handkerchief soaked in vaginal fluid, a vintage digital of Irina hanging out panties on the washing line, stretching up on her lustful tiptoes?'

Roberto told her they had discussed her anatomical particulars.

He was referring to the darkest speck of skin peeking out from the bottom of her breast, I instantly recalled the way it felt rough on my tongue.

'The little voice inside me that lives for winning arguments was one step away from snapping back that, after he'd shown him my collection of semi-naked photos, being in possession of that information wasn't exactly conclusive evidence. But they're stronger, they have conviction, throw more weight behind their words, it never does us any favours, I wasn't going to get out of this by having a conversation, so I stayed quiet. Roberto went straight to the handbook:

"Why didn't you tell me?"

"You cheated on me."

"What else are you hiding from me?"

'He cornered me. I told him the first thing that came to mind. I told him about you. I told him that when you started sleeping with guys, it wasn't just comforting that you told me, it was fun, I told him that we decided not to have secrets, not like that, that we cleared that channel of communication that so often gets blocked with mixed feelings and narrow thinking. I told him that we cleansed our skin of jealousy, I think I even told him that jealousy is a mental illness, a straitjacket for the flesh. I was having a philosophical night, I never find that sweet spot when I write my scripts. What I can't forget is his face (shock, disgust, hunger, the certainty that he wouldn't dare) when he heard the story that some of your guys wanted to go to bed with both of us.'

They agreed to sleep with other people, flirted with new partners, Irina was the first to get on board. She was the least inhibited of the two, she had the nerve to approach people and I guess it's always easier for women to find men who're up for it, especially if you're not too fussy about personality.

She leaned back in her chair. In school, she had liked to keep stirring the tiny spoon in her coffee long after the sugar had dissolved; she made me laugh when she came out of Nico's house, exaggeratedly complimenting the boy's enthusiasm for choosing air freshener. She would stand up from a restaurant table and demand, to a round of applause, that the pastry chef come out of the kitchen so she could congratulate them. In museums, she would make fun of the exhibits:

"They're like suburban bedrooms. My aunt has one just like that in Santa Coloma."

If anyone sat next to us on the metro, Irina couldn't stay quiet for a second:

"Next week he's taking me to Tehran to meet his parents. Here you get so much hassle about female circumcision. We've got tickets for a burka fashion show."

We fooled around a lot, she always made me laugh with the things she said; when we said goodbye, I'd watch her skipping away; she hated the rain, three drops would be enough to make her run for cover. She made fun of me when I suggested getting out of Barcelona, the mountains bored her, after one glance she'd be tired of the view, she said you couldn't do anything with a tree; she complained she had myrmecophobia. She'd wait for me at the door of the Auditori or the Mélies in jeans and a t-shirt, slowly moving her tongue around her mouth. After we made love she'd go to the fridge: cherries, grapes, cookies; she'd phone the Chinese place and order enough food to have leftovers; even with a plate between her legs, she never got tired of touching me. She'd throw her head back when she laughed; she spent August nights submerged in the bath and walked around the flat with her skin wet; we watched BBC comedy series, classic episodes of *Doctor Who*. The extension of that girl with the narrow hips and comic talent was right there in front of me with a lump in her throat, and I didn't really know what to make of her.

'What I didn't tell him is that there's no guarantee that these petty feelings would go away, and it wasn't entirely clear that they were petty. What I didn't tell him is that I was trapped in an idea of adventure that wasn't for me, that those forays of ours felt like someone was stealing our love, like a little humiliation I was bringing on myself so that I wouldn't lose ground, so that you wouldn't drop me out of your life. What I didn't tell him was that excitement lights us up like lamps but you can't let those messed up ideas run your life, it's not about opening my mind more, my mind couldn't be any more open, it tugs at strings that are just too delicate, you can't do that. What I didn't tell him is that I just wanted you, and you left.'

I think I said: 'I'm sorry'.

Yes, that's what I said.

'I played my part. I told him every detail of every encounter. It didn't help that something started moving in his underpants.'

When they slept together, they went beyond what had been agreed, the aggression spilled over to outside the bed.

'He clenches his fists and bends his knees and he screams; sorry, when I think about it out of context it kind of makes me laugh.'

She stopped telling him. She stopped trying. What was broken could not be fixed. They kept on acting like a couple, trying not to cross paths.

'He looks down on me because I took his bullshit seriously. And so I let him pound me from behind, where I don't get to see his eyes, and encourage him to massage my breasts, when they start to hurt I know he's about to finish, dirty talk helps him. He asks for it. I give it to him. It's no trouble. Afterwards, I look at him, I think about smoking, I think about how someone new, really new, would see this room, what things they would move around. For the last three months, I've been secretly seeing other men. Two, they came along at almost the same time. Roberto suspects, but he suspected before. I try to satisfy them, we're careful not to leave marks, I enjoy watching them wash themselves so thoroughly, even though their clean skin is for another woman. Some afternoons they turn me on like before, I don't expect it, I don't demand it, I can't get the idea out of my head that I'm acting. Reality is the thing I can't fix with my man, what's still there when you close your eyes and think about it differently. I guess it helps to think that he goes with other women too, and we're somehow staying loyal in our minds. I imagine we'll keep fucking in different beds until the bitterness wins out and we can split up.'

Notes

1. Catalan for newcomers.

About the Editors

Manel Ollé is a lecturer in History and Culture of Contemporary China at the Pompeu Fabra University of Barcelona (UPF). His published works include *Made in China: el despertar social, político y cultural de la China contemporánea* (2005) and *La Xina que arriba: perspectives del segle XXI* (2009). He writes literary criticism and has translated the work of Li Qingzhao and Gao Xingjian among others. He is also a poet and was awarded the Gabriel Ferrater Prize for Poetry for his collection *Bratislava o Bucarest* (2014), and the 2021 Jocs Florals de Barcelona for his poem 'Un grapat de pedres d'aigua' (A Handful of Water Stones).

Zoë Turner graduated from Manchester Metropolitan University with a BA in English Literature. She went on to complete a Masters in Film and Television: Research and Production at the University of Birmingham. She has run workshops to encourage community engagement with short form writing, and has worked alongside organisations such as Ort Gallery and The Barber Institute of Fine Arts to create films for digital engagement. She is an editor and publicist at Comma Press, as well as fiction editor for the online feminist magazine *The F-Word*.

About the Authors

Born in 1982, **Borja Bagunyà** has published three short story collections, *Apunts per al retrat d'una ciutat* (Arola, 2004), *Defensa pròpia* (Premi Mercè Rodoreda, 2006) and *Plantes d'interior* (Empuries, 2010). His stories have appeared in the anthologies *Voices* (Empúries, 2010) and *Risc* (Rata_Books, 2017). He teaches Comparative Literature at the University of Barcelona. In 2016, he cofounded Escola Bloom with Lana Bastasic.

Carlota Gurt is a writer and translator. She has translated work by Nino Haratischwili, Hans Magnus Enzensberger, Peter Handke, Sarah Lark, and David Safier, and was previously production manager for La Fura dels Baus and the Temporada Alta Festival. Her first collection of short stories, *Cavalcarem tota la nit* (2019) won the Mercè Rodoreda Prize.

Empar Moliner burst onto the Catalan and Spanish literary scene in 1999 with her book, *L'ensenyador de pisos que odiava els mims*, a collection of satirical stories offering sarcastic and sometimes shocking perspectives on everyday obsession. Her first novel, *Feli, esthéticienne*, a comic account of passion, was awarded the prominent Josep Pla Prize in 2000. Her collection of stories, *T'estimo si he begut* was awarded the most influential Catalan literary prize, the Lletra d'Or Prize, and was voted the book of the year by *La Vanguardia* and *El Periódico* magazines. The English edition, *I Love You When I'm Drunk*, was published by Comma Press in 2008. She currently works as a writer and journalist.

Jordi Nopca is a Spanish journalist, writer and translator. He is currently editor of *Ara* newspaper and the editor-in-chief of *Ara Llegim*.

Marta Orriols is a Catalan writer based in Barcelona. After studying history of art, she studied screenwriting at the Bande à Part Film School in Barcelona and then creative writing at the Escola d'Escriptura de l'Ateneu Barcelonès, which led her to debut collection of short stories *Anatomia de les distàncies curtes* (2016). Her first novel *Aprendre a parlar amb les plantes* was awarded the Òmnium Cultural Prize for the best Catalan novel, and was followed in 2020, with a second *Dolça introducció al caos*. Her novels have been translated into several languages, including English (*Learning to Talk to Plants*, published by Pushkin Press). She occasionally works as an editorial reader and is a contributor to several newspapers and magazines.

Jordi Puntí was born in 1967 and lives in Barcelona. He has published three books of short stories: *Pell d'armadillo*, *Animals tristos* and *Això no és Amèrica*, which came out in English as *This Is Not America* (Atria Books, 2018). In 2010, he published his first novel, *Maletes perdudes,* also translated into English as *Lost Luggage* (Short Books), which received the National Critics' Award, the Booksellers Award, and has been translated into 18 languages. He is also the author of *Els castellans*, an autobiographical fiction. His most recent book is *Messi: Lessons in style* (Short Books, 2018), a literary and sentimental portrait of one of the world's greatest footballers. He is a contributor to *El Periódico* newspaper, the cultural magazine *L'Avenç*, and a radio show about literature, *Ciutat Maragda*. In 2014 he was a recipient of the prestigious fellowship for the Cullman Center for Scholars and Writers, at the New York Public Library, for a novel project which is in progress.

Llucia Ramis is a Catalan language journalist and writer. She studied journalism at Universitat Autònoma de Barcelona, and has worked in different media, including the newspaper *Diario de Mallorca*, the literary magazine *Quimera*, COM Ràdio, Rac1 and the Catalan edition of *El Mundo* newspaper.

Francesc Seres is a Catalan writer, born in Saidi, Aragon in 1972. He studied fine art and anthropology at the Universitat de Barcelona and now works as a professor of art history. His novels, short stories and plays have been translated into Spanish and other European languages.

Gonzalo Torné was born in Barcelona in 1976. He has published four novels: *Divorce is in the air* (Knopf / Harvill, 2013), *Hilos de sangre* (2010), *Años felices* (2017) and *El corazón de la fiesta* (2020).

Carlos Zanón is the author of four volumes of poetry and three novels, which have received wide critical acclaim in Spain. *The Barcelona Brothers* is his first novel to be published in English. A literary critic and screenwriter, he has also collaborated as a lyricist for rock bands. He lives in Barcelona.

About the Translators

Jennifer Arnold is a lecturer in Spanish and Translation Studies at Newcastle University. She is a literary translator from Catalan and Spanish and was awarded the Emerging Translator Mentorship for Catalan with Peter Bush by the National Centre for Writing in 2016. She has published translations of works by Tina Valles and Maria Zambrano, and translated poetry by Noelia Diaz-Vicedo. She has also recently organized a series of talks and seminars around the theme of Reading in Translation which can be found at https://www.facebook.com/readingacrosscultures:

Helena Buffery teaches and researches at University College Cork, with a special focus on translation, contemporary Iberian Studies and Spanish and Latin American theatre and performance. She has published widely on different aspects of Catalan culture, including translations of *The Book of Deeds of James I of Aragon* (2003, with Damian Smith) and Maria-Mercè Marçal's *La passió segons Renée Vivien* (2020, with Kathleen McNerney).

Peter Bush's first literary translation was Juan Goytisolo's *Forbidden Territory* and he has translated eleven other books by this writer, including *The Marx Family Saga* and *Exiled from Almost Everywhere*. He has translated a number of classics: from Spanish, Fernando de Roja's *Celestina* and Pedro Alarcón's *The Three-Cornered Hat*; from Catalan, Mercè Rodoreda's *In Diamond Square*, Joan Sales' *Uncertain Glory* and Josep Pla's *The Gray Notebook*, *Life Embitters* and *Salt Water*; from French, Balzac's *The Lily in the Valley* and is now working on Proust's

The Guermantes Way. He has recently translated fiction by Najat El Hachmi, Quim Monzó, Teresa Solana and Jorge Carrión. He is a former Director of the British Centre for Literary Translation.

Ruth Clarke is a translator from Spanish, French and Italian. She has translated an eclectic range of work by authors from Benin to Venezuela, including Cristina Caboni's debut novel *The Secret Ways of Perfume* and Aurora Lassaletta Atienza's *The Invisible Brain Injury*. Her latest translation is Evelina Santangelo's novel *From Another World*, published by Granta. Ruth is a founding member of The Starling Bureau, a collective of literary translators.

Mara Faye Lethem is an award-winning translator of contemporary Catalan and Spanish prose, and the author of *A Person's A Person, No Matter How Small*. Her recent translations include books by Patricio Pron, Max Besora, Javier Calvo, Marta Orriols, Toni Sala, Alicia Kopf, and Irene Solà. She is currently working on the collected short stories of Pere Calders.

Annie McDermott's translations from Spanish and Portuguese include *Dead Girls* and *Brickmakers* by Selva Almada, *Empty Words* and *The Luminous Novel* by Mario Levrero, *Wars of the Interior* by Joseph Zárate and *City of Ulysses* by Teolinda Gersão (co-translation with Jethro Soutar). She has previously lived in Mexico City and São Paulo, Brazil, and is now based in Hastings.

Laura McGloughlin has been a freelance translator from Catalan and Spanish since completing a Masters in literary translation at the University of East Anglia. She was awarded the inaugural British Centre for Literary Translation Catalan-